FUTURISTIC CANADA

FUTURISTIC CANADA

JF GARRARD
SARAH WATERRAVEN

Copyright © 2019 by Dark Helix Press

All rights reserved.

No part of this book may be reproduced in any form or by any electronic or mechanical means, including information storage and retrieval systems, without written permission from the publisher/author, except for the use of brief quotations in a book review.

Dark Helix Press books are published by Dark Helix Press Inc.

darkhelixpress.com

Print ISBN: 978-1-988416-21-2

E-book ISBN: 978-1-988416-22-9

Library and Archives Canada Cataloguing in Publication

Title: Futuristic Canada / edited by JF Garrard & Sarah WaterRaven.

Names: Garrard, J. F., 1978- editor. | WaterRaven, Sarah, editor.

Identifiers: Canadiana (print) 20190090405 | Canadiana (ebook) 20190090421 | ISBN 9781988416212

(softcover) | ISBN 9781988416229 (PDF)

Subjects: CSH: Speculative fiction, Canadian (English)

Classification: LCC PS8323.S3 F88 2019 | DDC C813/.08760806—dc23

To our Families

CONTENTS

Introduction — ix

1. Sell off by Mathias Jansson — 1
2. Here Comes Santa Claus by Andrew Jensen — 3
3. Carnaval Stream by Christine Rains — 17
4. Making Waves by Frederick Charles Melancon — 23
5. The Night Librarian by Helen Power — 33
6. Carbon Concerns by Ryan Toxopeus — 47
7. Her Last Walk by Paul Williams — 55
8. Mother of the Caribou By Christine Rains — 63
9. Space and Time Books by Melissa Yuan-Innes — 67
10. Abootasaurus! By Timothy Carter — 75
11. Canadian Gods by Ira Nayman — 89
12. Protecting Artifacts in Hebes Chasma by Frederick Charles Melancon — 101
13. Medically Necessary by Andrew Jensen — 107
14. Lingua Franca by Jen Frankel — 121
15. Designing Fate by JF Garrard — 125
16. Poutine, Bugs and Big Bessie by Melissa Small — 143

About the Editors & Authors — 159

INTRODUCTION

O Canada!
Our home and native land!
True patriot love in all of us command.

Canada recently celebrated its one hundred and fiftieth anniversary in the year 2017! Canada has gone through many changes this last century and seen great progress, but with problems like global warming, political unrest, and social discord in neighboring countries, many of us find ourselves questioning the future.

What will Canada be like in another one hundred and fifty years? Will our values and good will triumph over our problems or will we face a strange apocalyptic future?

Fiction is written to entertain, to inform, and to persuade. The authors in this book all share their visions of a Futuristic Canada. Some of the stories presented here are warnings about how dire the future can become, while others carry messages of hope. The common thread in all stories is to persuade us to think about and be aware of the impacts of our own actions in this world. As Mahatma Gandhi says, "Be the change that you wish to see in the world."

We hope that you will enjoy these stories in front of a warm fire on a snowy night or by a lake on a sunny day!

Best,
> JF & SW

SELL OFF BY MATHIAS JANSSON

After the bankruptcy
    we bought it all
    all below the Niagara Falls
the remaining Great Lakes
the Grand Canyon
and the Key West.
Yes, we bought it all
except the great wall.

We then expatriated all the
    corrupted politicians and racists
    to the volcanic island in the Pacific.
    We used all the empty land
    to build a pure energy park
    with solar panel and windmills
    so we could cool down
    all Las Vegas casinos
    into palaces for ice hockey.

. . .

And New York changed
>   into a fantastic place
>   a wildlife reserve
>   with wolves on Wall Street
>   beavers in Bronx
>   and of course Grizzly Bears
>   in Central Park.

But best of all
>   we painted the White House red and white
>   and then resculpted the Rushmore cliff
>   into a giant maple leaf.
>   Yes, we bought it all
>   so our neighbours could
>   enjoy something new
>   a feeling we in Canada call freedom.

2

HERE COMES SANTA CLAUS BY ANDREW JENSEN

Originally Published in *Midnight Zoo* Magazine,
Vol. 2, Issue #5, Christmas 1992

David Stewart rode slowly through the town. He looked it over carefully as he followed the main street, noting his first impressions. Many of the homes were made of the yellow brick people in the region called "white." They were not fancy but seemed to be in good repair. Some lots were vacant, but none would be considered derelict. Most had vegetable gardens. It was late fall, and there were plenty of tomatoes in sight, but even with the extended growing season caused by climate change, they wouldn't last much longer. Plants needed light and the days were growing shorter.

His first impressions were enough to make him curious. He could see that the people here were poor, which was no surprise since a great many small Ontario towns had sunk into poverty. After the pandemic, and the collapse of the economy, very few small towns had much to trade. But New Jericho did not seem depressed in any way. The sign welcoming him to town was newly painted. David couldn't see any idle adults, and he was happily aware that this town didn't have the automatic hostile stare he'd come to expect as a stranger. No one had welcomed him, exactly, but he didn't feel any hostility, either. The only building he could see which had decayed past repair was being systematically torn down by six men. Actually, one man and five teenagers. And with the coveralls they all wore, he couldn't tell anyone's gender, beyond the full beard of the leader. The yellow bricks they had already removed were clean of all mortar and were neatly stacked in front of the house next door, ready for reuse. The workers seemed purposeful and cooperative.

His horse, already walking slowly, came to a complete stop. A small girl stood right in his path. He noticed her plain summer dress, obviously homemade and repaired enough to suggest that this child had a thrifty and caring family. David smiled ruefully, thinking that when he had been a child, such clothes would never have been seen in late November. Global warming had banished the snowy winters he used to enjoy.

The girl took his smile for a good omen. She smiled at him and said, "You're a Stranger, aren't you?"

He replied, "Yes, I am. I'm David Stewart. Do you know where the Mayor is?"

The girl looked his horse over with a practised eye.

"We have a mare, but your horse is a gelding. They don't care about mares."

David was confused for a moment. Before he could rephrase his question, the girl asked, "Have you seen the Elders yet?"

Elders! David sat up straighter. This might prove to be a very fruitful visit. "No," he said. "Where can I find them?"

"I'm not allowed to talk to Strangers who haven't seen the Elders yet," said the girl. She started to back away.

"Tell me where they are, and I'll go see them right away."

The girl shook her head and continued to back away.

"You don't need to talk," David called. "Just point."

The girl pointed. There were a few large buildings a couple of blocks ahead. One was more imposing than the others and made of the more expensive red bricks.

"Should I go to the big red building?" David called.

The girl nodded. Then she turned and scooted behind a house.

Elders! David poked his horse into a faster walk than before. If the change from "town councillor" to "elder" meant what he hoped, then he could accomplish quite a bit here.

David hitched his horse to the post at the town hall and went inside. In a sparsely furnished office, he was met by a small woman with white hair.

"How can I help you, Stranger?" she asked kindly.

"My name is David Stewart," he said. "I'd like to speak to one of the Elders."

"I'm Elder Rosie McLachlan," the woman replied. "Today is my turn in the office. How may I help you?"

"I'm a theology student, working on my Ph.D. thesis. It's about the different ways the change in society has affected traditional forms of faith. I'm particularly interested in new expressions of the Reformed tradition. I'm a Presbyterian, myself." David didn't mention that his thesis advisor called his research "cult crawling."

Rose was silent for a moment. Then, frowning slightly, she asked, "You mean you just want to learn what we believe? Come to church and talk to us; things like that?"

"Yes. I'd like to stay for a week or two and interview people, especially the Elders. If I could attend worship with you, that would be a great help."

"You promise not to do any preaching, or try to change what any of us believe?"

"I promise!" David replied emphatically. "I want to learn what you believe now. Changing that would be the worst thing I could do."

Rose McLachlan smiled. "We agree about that. Well, you're welcome to stay with us. The Bible enjoins us to welcome Strangers, and we do, but we expect you to respect our ways while you're here."

"Are there any particular rules I should know about?" he asked.

"If you've studied the Bible, as you say you have, you'll know them all. The Bible is the guide to everything we do. You'll catch on quickly." She smiled, then added, "Unless you're wealthy. If you are, keep it to yourself. We expect you to pay your way, of course, but don't be too free with your money. We're not a well-off town by old standards, and we've learned the hard way that the love of money is evil. *Do not* lead anyone into temptation."

"I'll be careful," David replied. He added to himself, *besides, I don't have that much myself.*

David's research went well, although it didn't turn up anything extraordinary. The town had experienced a religious revival when the national economy collapsed. The local United Church had strong Presbyterian roots, so the revival took a Reformed shape, with a heavy emphasis on the Bible. The whole town, as well as the surrounding farms, had become a single religious community, ruled by the church Elders. They acted as both lawmakers and court when the need arose.

Sunday worship was like going back in time two hundred years, to the 1880s. All signs of wealth or decoration had been stripped from the church; even the stained-glass windows had been replaced by plain or frosted glass, and even some of those were gone, replaced by neatly cut boards. David noted too that there weren't any offering plates in evidence. He decided to ask about this when he spoke to his next interviewee.

The man in question was quite old, although not an official Elder. David suspected the roguish twinkle in the old fellow's eyes kept him from being considered responsible enough.

"We haven't passed the plate for years," he explained. "No one has anything to put in it. If something needs doing, we just do it. If we had a minister to support, there'd be a problem, but the Elders take turns preaching." He grinned. "For free!"

David grinned back. Some things didn't change. "I just have one more question. You were around when the town was re-named New Jericho. Why did you folks choose that particular name?"

The man's grin widened. "'Cause the walls were a-tumblin' down."

Shortly before the end of his second week in New Jericho, David was summoned before a meeting of the Elders. The senior Elder, Henry van Erp, addressed him formally.

"Mr. Stewart, for the most part, you've been a welcome guest. You've refrained from directly preaching your beliefs, and have mostly respected our ways. However, a problem has come to our attention. It concerns your wealth. Rose McLachlan said that she specifically warned you not to flaunt any wealth here. Yet you've done just that. On many occasions you've openly used an electrical device: a voice recorder, I believe. This has caused discontent among the young people."

David was stunned. He *had* brought a small digital recorder, several memory cards, and a solar-powered battery charger for his interviews. He hadn't dreamed it would become a problem.

"But it's only a digital recorder," he protested.

"Mr. Stewart," continued van Erp, "a digital recorder isn't a small thing. You have noticed, I'm sure, that there are no electrical devices of any sort in New Jericho."

David had noticed, without much surprise. Few small towns could afford the cost of electricity unless they could generate their own.

"This isn't just because we can't afford it. We chose to abandon these things and the other wasteful parts of the old, corrupt society that rotted and collapsed years ago. Your recorder seems innocuous, and you're friendly and polite. Some of our young folk are wondering whether the old ways were really so bad. The Devil takes many forms, and the most dangerous appears to be the most innocent.

"Mr. Stewart, our youngest children have never even seen a snowman. They'll never know the extinct animals. They hear us talk, but they'll never really know what they're missing. They're paying for the sins of their parents. That is not 'only' a recorder. It's a threat. So are you. It is the decision of the Elders that you must leave New Jericho at first light tomorrow."

David was horrified. His best source of material in two years of travelling was throwing him out. He had to salvage something.

"Elders," he said, "I'm very sorry for this trouble. I had no idea this would be a problem. If I'd understood your beliefs, I would never have used my recorder. My work isn't finished. Another five days would be enough. Please let me stay that long. I'll put away the recorder, or even destroy it in public if that would help undo the damage I've caused. Without the machine, I wouldn't be any kind of a threat to your teachings. I'll abide by whatever decision you make, or whatever restrictions you put on me. But please, I ask of you, allow me to stay just a few more days to finish my work."

Van Erp looked around at the other Elders, and then back at David. "We'll consider your request. Please wait outside."

David waited over an hour for their decision. As he secretly looked at his watch, he considered what he was experiencing. On the one hand, he was witnessing how deeply their faith controlled their daily lives, and how they dealt with problems: banish sinners, keep the town separate and pure. On the other hand, it looked like he wouldn't be able to stay long enough to expand on this new knowledge. The long discussion gave him hope, though. Clearly, they were not unanimous about sending him away.

At last, he was invited back into the room.

"Mr. Stewart," van Erp said, "we've considered your request for more time and we've decided that you can do more to repair the damage you've caused by staying than by leaving. You may stay the five days you requested, and possibly longer, if things go well."

David couldn't help but grin in relief.

"There are some conditions, of course," the Elder continued. "You must leave your digital recorder with us. We'll return it to you when you depart. Curiosity has arisen among the younger folk concerning Toronto, where I understand you lived, and the other places you've visited. You may not speak of these things to anyone under the age of forty. Older residents have their own memories to weigh against your words. I don't think you'll have much opportunity to speak to the children. We don't forbid you from speaking to them, but their parents will probably warn them away from you. Do *not* encourage them in any way to disobey their parents."

Van Erp went on to describe further conditions, which included moving into a basement room in the town hall since his host family would undoubtedly ask him to leave. The conditions were strict, but at least he could stay. He felt a bit like a leper but was pleased his work could continue.

As van Erp spoke, David looked around at the faces of the other Elders. As he had expected, this had not been a unanimous decision—that much was clear from the expressions on various faces. It did seem odd, though, that the Elders who had been the most cooperative during his interviews now seemed the most unhappy with his staying.

The next few days passed without incident. David was so busy gathering information and taking notes by hand that he only occasionally noticed the way that children, and some adults, were avoiding him. It was an uncomfortable way to live, but it gave him new insights for his thesis.

On the fourth day of his reprieve, David was approached by one of the younger Elders, Bill Smith, with a proposal that delighted him. He was asked to take part in a celebration.

"I'd be honoured," David said. "Can you tell me a little more about it?"

Bill looked a little embarrassed. "Actually, it's a Santa Claus parade. Tomorrow is December 6th, which is St. Nicholas' Day, and that's when we have our parade."

David was surprised. "Santa Claus? He's not exactly a religious figure, at least, that's not the way he came across in the parades I remember from my childhood."

Bill shook his head. "No, sir. We've added some real meaning to the parade. It may look the same at first, but by the end, you'll see the deeper meaning. You won't have to do much. You dress up as Santa and throw presents from your wagon to the children. The kids really love this parade."

David was frankly curious. "Of course I'll play Santa for

you. I'd give anything to see how this works out. To be honest, Santa seems much too secular to fit in here."

Bill smiled knowingly. "I guess it looks that way to an outsider. Actually, you're lucky. Only one Stranger per year is allowed to be in New Jericho for the Santa Claus Parade."

David became concerned. "Will I be allowed to write about this in my thesis? I wouldn't want to break any rules, but this may prove to be one of the most interesting parts of my work."

Bill smiled again. "We discussed that very question just this morning. None of the Elders are worried about this appearing in your work. It might be hard to take notes while you're playing Santa Claus. But don't worry about that, these parades are hard to forget."

David didn't doubt that. For people whose lives were as bare and restricted as this, any kind of celebration must be memorable. He was looking forward to the next day. He wanted to see how such repressed people behaved when they partied.

The next morning, David and his horse reported to Bill Smith's house at the edge of town. There, David was fitted out with an old white toque which had been inexpertly dyed red, the remains of an old wool sweater that had been transformed into an almost white beard, and a vintage red jacket, several sizes too big, from which someone had carefully removed the name "McGill." It seemed odd that the Santa for the parade should be dressed so shabbily. Usually, for a celebration, people try to produce their best. This looked like a deliberate attempt to make it look like the worst.

Perhaps this was part of their symbolism: that even Santa Claus was impoverished? Spiritually impoverished? He decided to ask Bill about it and went over to where the young Elder was busy hooking up David's horse to the old wagon that would carry him.

"We had a real sleigh when I was a child," Bill remarked cheerfully. "But then the snow got so that you couldn't count on it. Now, it would be a miracle if it ever snowed before February."

David tried to ask about the symbolism behind the shabby costume, but Bill just shook his head impatiently.

"No time for that now," he said. "The children are waiting downtown. Just climb into the wagon and ride 'er down toward the town hall. You can throw the presents to the children as you go by them. And make sure the 'Ho, Ho, Hos' are nice and loud."

"Won't the presents be damaged if I throw them?"

Bill laughed. "Naw, they're just empty boxes with fancy paper. We'll use them again next year."

David asked, "Won't the children be disappointed?"

Bill grinned. "How could they be? They've never been thrown a real present. They love it just the way it is. You'll see. Now get going. They're waiting."

David got the horse and wagon going, and headed down the main street. He saw the crowds waiting just a few blocks ahead, neatly at the edges of the road, as if this were a real parade. He heard the sound of excited voices becoming louder as he approached. It looked as if the whole countryside had joined the town for the event. Children darted across the empty street as if it were the most daring thing they'd ever done, only to be scolded by adults when they crossed. Despite the fact that David couldn't see anyone in charge, everyone stayed back from the street. Couldn't these people let their hair down at all? He'd just have to do his best to liven things up. After all, he was the star of the show!

He opened the sack on the floor of the wagon. It was full of brightly wrapped boxes, each tied with a red ribbon. A few looked a bit scuffled and battered, obviously veterans of previous parades. He wasn't surprised that the boxes were reused. The wrapping and ribbon on each box looked like it was worth more than his whole Santa suit.

David carefully tossed one of the boxes to the closest child. He didn't want to ruin the colourful paper by letting it hit the ground, so he threw it straight to the child. He was astonished to see the young boy shriek and dodge aside from the "present."

It didn't take long for him to notice that all of the children behaved the same way. Each one would run from the parcels, yelling with delighted terror. He then observed that the children he had passed were following along behind the wagon, laughing and shouting in the middle of the street. Some of what he heard wasn't very civil.

They're rejecting him, David suddenly realized. *Santa is a symbol of greed and sin to them. They're teaching the children to fear and reject materialism!* David grinned. If the Elders had asked him to do this as a way of embarrassing him for the recorder business, then he would play along. He would play his part to the hilt.

"Ho! Ho! Ho!" he bellowed over the noise of the crowd. "Merry Christmas!"

David's words stopped suddenly as something hit him on the back. He reached behind the seat and picked up one of the empty boxes. It hadn't hurt, but he felt odd that it had happened at all. He looked back at the children behind the wagon. They were shouting and jeering now, with less mirth than before. One or two seemed to be preparing to throw other presents. David urged his horse to speed up.

The extra speed didn't last long. Santa David's way was blocked by a crowd of adults. Leading them was the chief Elder, Henry van Erp. He was dressed in the black robes and long preaching tabs of a nineteenth-century Presbyterian minister. While someone held the horse's bridle, van Erp climbed up into the wagon, carrying a heavy pulpit Bible, and stood next to the seated Santa.

"Santa Claus has come into our midst," van Erp intoned. "What does he bring?"

"Empty gifts!" shouted the crowd.

"Ho! Ho! Ho!" retorted David. The angry looks from the crowd made him wish he hadn't.

"What does Santa bring?" repeated van Erp.

"Empty promises!" the shout was louder.

"Is Santa good?" continued the robed Elder.

"No! No! No!"

"Is Santa holy?"

"No! No! No!"

"What does Santa bring to our Saviour's birth?"

"Mockery! Mockery!" The shout was deafening.

"What does Santa teach us?"

"Greed! Greed!"

David was no longer fascinated with this litany. The roar of the crowd was beginning to sound dangerous.

"What does Santa bring us?"

"Sin! Sin!"

"What do we need instead?"

"Food! Food!"

David was surprised at this nonspiritual answer.

"Then food you shall have!" Van Erp gestured at the horse, and David heard it scream in pain. Someone had expertly cut open the animal's throat, and its blood quickly pumped out onto the road.

The horse's scream snapped the fascination that had held David spellbound. He started up out of the wagon seat, a cry of outrage on his lips. Before he could utter anything coherent, his shout was cut off by the weight of a large Bible hitting his head.

Stunned and confused, David didn't resist as he was pulled down from the wagon. He barely noticed his hands being tied behind his back. He stumbled along past those who were carving up the dead horse and was led to an old parking lot behind the town hall. His wits began to return as he crossed the crumbling asphalt. He realized that the crowd was now rhythmically chanting:

Remember, remember, the sixth of December; Santa's a treasonous plot!

David shook his head in confusion. The chant was wrong. It should be November. And where was the gunpowder?

He felt himself being tied to a post. Then he noticed that each person in the crowd placed a piece of wood at his feet. As the pile grew higher, he observed that each piece was neatly tied with a red ribbon.

David tried to say something, but his miserable beard was tied into his mouth as a gag. He looked around desperately, and found van Erp, still in his minister's garb.

Something was wrong with that attire, too. The pair of white tabs representing the tablets of the Ten Commandments were too large, more like the kind worn by lawyers than preachers. The collar was wrong, too. Instead of the back-closing collar of the clergy, van Erp was wearing a front-closing collar. He wasn't dressed as a nineteenth-century minster. Van Erp was dressed as a nineteenth-century judge.

He began to speak, and the chanting crowd grew silent. "The scriptures tell us that we must put away our sin and purge our nation of evil. The scriptures tell us that a man who has sinned greatly should have his body delivered to Satan, that his soul may be saved, though tested by fire. Santa Claus once led a whole world to sin and destruction. We repudiate him and all his works. And he shall wear the sign of his sin, as a reminder to us all never to follow him."

At these words, Bill Smith came forward. He was smiling broadly, as always, but his eyes were too intense to be reassuring. David saw he was carrying the infamous voice recorder, neatly tied with a long loop of red ribbon. Bill reached up and hung the loop around David's neck, so the recorder hung at the centre of David's chest. As he did this, he whispered, "Thanks, David. You're the best Santa we've had in a long time." Then he stepped back.

The judge stepped forward. Someone had given him a burning torch, which he held in his left hand. The large Bible was in his right. Van Erp's voice boomed: "Thus do we purify ourselves." He cast the torch onto the pile of wood.

The celebration began as Santa burned.

3

CARNAVAL STREAM BY CHRISTINE RAINS

The rest of the country schedules their snow for Christmas, but Québec City reserves it for Carnaval. It's what brings the magic to the two week long winter festival. Or at least that's what I've always believed.

I stuffed my hands into my coat pockets as I wove through the crowd. Fat snowflakes covered trees and heads alike. A trio of kids ran by and splashed one of my legs with slush. Shivers drew my arms tighter to me as the wet cold soaked through my leggings and bit at my skin.

My older sister Karelle said the snow was for the corporations. They controlled most aspects of people's lives these days. Our schooling, our diets, the government. So why not the weather too? When it's snowing nowhere else in the world, it attracts loads of tourists. I hated that she was right. Despite my more advanced implants, she was the smarter one. Probably why she was chosen as one of the seven Duchesses this year.

Anséline, we're about ten meters ahead to the left.

I picked up my pace and smiled at hearing Henri's voice over my PsiNet. I nearly slipped as the distance in steps flashed in front of my left eye. I ignored the stream of data and relished seeing my friends out of the Net. I hadn't seen them since the holidays, and while that was less than two months ago, it seemed a long time, especially since I grew up seeing them at school every day.

My friends stood off to one side of the walkway, huddled together near a lamp post. Gisele said something and everyone laughed. I picked up my pace.

"Henri!" I rushed up and hugged him, then kissed each of his cheeks. My surface thoughts echoed onto my Stream as I exclaimed how excited I was to see him.

He gave me a squeeze, flattening his puffy jacket. His Stream echoed his happiness seeing me. "It's been too long. You just *had* to go to Vancouver for school."

I nudged him and laughed. "I was home at Christmas."

"Too long." Therese agreed and nabbed me for a hug.

I gave her polite kisses but didn't note her on my Stream. She'd been contracted as a compatible companion by their corporation to Henri for one year, but in September, he'd be single again. Six months, nine days. I had a private counter ticking away the minutes in my database.

"So nice to see you again, Therese." I greeted Gisele and Lazare, friends I'd known since grade school. I'd known Henri just as long, but because he was Lazare's older brother by two years.

"You're coming over for meatball stew later, right?" Gisele's tiny nose crinkled with her smile.

Of course she is. She always hogs the meatballs. Lazare didn't move his mouth. Rarely did he actually speak anymore. He claimed PsiNet made mouths obsolete.

I laughed and stuck my tongue out at him.

"You must be so thrilled about your sister being one of the Duchesses this year." Therese sighed and glanced at the ice palace. "Maybe one year I'll be chosen."

I deleted all the sarcastic responses that popped up. What I needed to do was be encouraging. Super encouraging. "It's exciting. I bet you'll make it next year or the year after. Not many people work in the archaeological sciences anymore, and with the ruins found on Mars, they could really use you there."

"You're perfect for the job." Henri grinned at his wife. *Contracted* wife. A relationship he agreed to just for business purposes. Did he want her gone as much as I did?

We chatted and laughed and threw snowballs at each other until it was time for the ceremony for the Dukes and Duchesses. Linking arms with Gisele, she and I led the way to the ice palace.

"Don't you have to be there with your family?" Therese snuggled into Henri.

I didn't look their way as I shook my head. "No. Just my parents and my brother. There's only room on the stage for so many." And they didn't want the artist of the family to embarrass them. Everyone in my family went into the sciences. Most of my friends were in the service industry. Me, I had other dreams. "You guys are stuck with me."

The ice palace grounds were packed. It didn't matter when the whole thing would feed live into the Stream. The snowflakes melted before they reached us here. I tugged up my hood and leaned against Gisele as I closed my eyes to focus on the Stream. The implants projected images in my eyes of the grand show happening on the stage.

The Duchesses and Dukes wore uniforms decorated with the symbols of each of the corporations that funded the Mars program. Nothing like the pretty fur coats they'd wear years ago. Though some folks still dressed in retro costumes in the many parades. Carnaval mirrored Mardi Gras in the south, but with ice, snow, and its jolly representative, Bonhomme. A snowman is more magical than Santa.

Speeches and applause. I tuned it out when Henri sent me a private message.

You seem out of sorts today. You okay?

His concern made me smile. *Karelle is going to Mars. That means my parents are going to have more time to bother me. Sometimes I wish I could just block them permanently.*

You don't mean that. They're nice folks, if a little pushy.

A little. Right. Besides, all I need is you guys.

We'll always be here for you. No matter where we are in the universe.

I jerked my head to the left to stare at him. *What do you mean?*

I meant that no matter where our lives take us—

I narrowed my eyes. *None of us are ever leaving Canada. We all swore it together in the ice palace when we were kids.*

Henri sighed. *Mars needs geotechnical engineers. Therese and I have been talking a lot about it. It would be a great move for my career.*

Therese, of course. I turned away and closed my eyes to contain my tears. Sure, Henri had always been career focused, but never the way my family was. He wouldn't push aside those he cared about for his job.

Anséline, don't be that way.

I'd block him if I could. I'd block the entire world.

You'll always be special to me. You're my best friend.

Special. Best friend. Seemed all my years of wishing and planning were for nil. None of my nanos could take away the ache in my chest.

Fireworks banged and snapped, signalling the end of the ceremony. The end of life as I knew it.

I tilted my head back and let my hood fall. Fat drops streamed down on my face. Even with all the whoops and cheers around me, the magic was gone. The corporations had taken that too. They'd taken him.

4

MAKING WAVES BY FREDERICK CHARLES MELANCON

At a cheap motel in Louisiana, Emily slammed her door in Louis's face. They'd only met through work about a week ago and hadn't been dating that long.

The vibrations along the door sent memories coursing through her: memories of the chocolate waters of the Bayou Teche. To many, the bayou on the far side of the motel was a stagnant body of water that slowly moved to God knows where, but those waters, rippling around reeds and framed by bearded oak trees, represented a first for Emily. The bayou, the only one she'd ever seen, amounted to an adventure.

She'd been a poor girl in Nova Scotia, and when her brother left all those years ago for a job in Toronto, she'd been abandoned. The morning that she'd woken up alone, she ran out to the Bay of Fundy and watched the water's annual escape into the Atlantic. The churn of water left behind jagged cliffs and a barren seabed that reminded her of the walls and empty beds in her house.

The bay had found an escape and she'd found one too.

She never wanted to be trapped by the choices of other people—her father or brother. She needed to flow freely and explore new places. Emily yearned to see where her current would take her. That morning, like tonight, she promised herself that she'd leave...

Two days ago, in a little park on the banks of Bayou Teche, Louis dug his hands into his machine. The device reminded Emily of a mechanical squid. From what she could tell, Louis worked on a rectangular box that made up the body. The eye was a single monitor that displayed test results and a multiple-cord sensor, attached to one side of the body, acted as its tentacles. The squid was designed to pick up energy signatures that people emitted and then display a visual on the monitor. Seemed simple, but the machine was heavy. Whenever the energy detector needed moving, they both worked together to carry it. Worse, the tentacles needed to be arrayed in such a way as to pick up a correct reading.

That information was vital for Emily's presence on the bayou. Mr. Voorhies, her new boss, was a politician involved in a nasty campaign in Canada. In a bid to erode his supporters, the opposing candidate questioned his French heritage. In a predominately French-speaking district, his approval ratings dropped along with his hopes for re-election. In fact, his numbers dropped so much that his analysts speculated that proving his heritage wouldn't be enough anymore. The idea for Emily's job came from that conversation. Of course, the boss's background was French and even included some of the Acadians from Nova Scotia who'd been forced by the British to immigrate, ending up in Southern Louisiana. If he could show that his energy matched his ancestors, he could not only prove his history, but he'd also become a victim in the eyes of the electorate, and his numbers would surely surge. Unfortunately, he couldn't take time off the campaign trail for a vacation. What would the voters think? That's where Emily came in.

Her French lineage was pristine, and Voorhies wanted Louis to test his device on her before the politician broadcasted it live during a campaign rally in Canada. So, the poor girl from North Grand Pré, and the scientist, teleported to the town in Louisiana that Voorhies' ancestors eventually called home; the two sharing particles before even appearing in St. Martinville.

It wasn't going well. On the first day of the job, with the sensor wires wrapped around Louis's uneven shoulders, he cursed.

"You're moving too much," Louis said.

Emily held her breathe. The memory of Louis's hands against her torso last night still flickered over her skin, but she didn't hold her breath just for him. Teleports weren't cheap, and the only reason for her paid vacation was Mr. Voorhies. He bought her ticket. His continued support allowed her to travel—to escape.

"You're not moving, are you?" Louis asked.

"I was breathing," Emily replied.

"Yeah, let's not stop that."

The wires slipped from his shoulders falling neatly into two separate piles as he stepped over the low hanging ropes that kept tourists from walking on the oak's roots. Displayed on the squid's screen was a dot with Louis's name above it, preceded by a red-coloured trail. Louis was an energy Casanova.

The way the machine worked was that auras could be matched, and by matching the colour of energy signatures already present in a certain location, the energy detector could prove anyone's ancestry. In Louis's case, his energy field remained vibrant. The hues of his aura surrounded Emily's dot, leaving a donut of black space.

"We could try the statue," Emily suggested.

"I need to call Voorhies," Louis said.

Emily felt as if she'd fallen into that black donut on the screen. At Voorhies's office in Toronto, she witnessed the colours she discharged. The deep purple she'd emitted matched her boss's perfectly. Nothing had changed on her way to Louisiana, so those waves still had to be there. There was the possibility that the machine wasn't working. If that were the case, Louis was supposed to call Voorhies. The boss's campaign covered only so much. If it wasn't going to work out, Voorhies intended to only pay Emily what she'd earned. But this was just the first day.

"What's wrong with you?" Louis asked the squid.

He was talking to the monitor, not her, but she didn't care if he was talking to the trees. "There's nothing wrong with me."

Later at the motel, she fiddled with the safety lock as she waited by her door for him. Voorhies paid for two separate rooms, but last night, Louis slept with her. Tonight, she fell asleep in a chair.

The next day, Louis didn't talk about the previous night. Instead, Louis informed Emily that Voorhies agreed with her, one day wasn't enough. And so, at a church located in the town square, Emily watched as Louis draped tentacles over the spokes of a wrought iron fence. The fence enclosed a small graveyard and a statue of Evangeline. Another statue of the same woman stood in front of a church just south of where Emily grew up in Grand Pré. The one Emily remembered from her childhood was sculpted to look as though Evangeline walked wistfully toward her lost love, and was not seated patiently, waiting on a pedestal like the one before her.

From what she remembered from school field trips to that church, Evangeline searched all over America to find the man that was ripped from her when they were forced to abandon their homes around 1755 by the British. When Evangeline had finally found him, he'd moved on and married some other girl.

In the heat, Emily tried to help. She arrayed the tentacles around the statue, while Louis spread them out on the fence. As Emily watched, her sweat sprinkled over Evangeline's feet, leaving tiny flecks of evaporating moisture. She kept her distance. Every time she touched the bronzed statue, her hands burned. Even Gabe, the local, who'd been enlisted to help them from the Visitor's Center, had a dark stain on his forearms from wiping the sweat off his round face.

Gabe had been Voorhies's idea. While only Louis's machine could trace energy signatures, Voorhies thought a local might show them forgotten places that Louis hadn't thought to survey. Louis argued with his boss about the unwanted help, but in the morning, Gabe had met them by the oaks with coffees in each hand. Without a sip, Louis dumped his in a nearby trashcan. Emily drank hers.

"All this for a poem," Gabe said.

"I never thought about it," Louis said.

"We know," Emily replied.

"Did you know that they tried to dig up the statue? Everyone thought the thing was a tombstone marker."

"We're using traces of people more than the statue," Emily informed him.

Gabe continued, "People were pretty upset. They believed the story was true."

"Walk around the statue, Em," Louis said.

Wondering when nicknames became a thing, Emily walked. The dot circled the screen without leaving a hint of colour. Louis stuck his head back in the machine. For a moment, the back of his shirt billowed from a gust of wind coming from a cooling fan. Filled with sweat, Emily's shirt itched as it stuck to the skin on her back.

"There's a state historic site on the north side of town. There's shade there," Gabe said.

"Shade's good," Emily said.

"I researched the place—too new," Louis said.

"If you don't like new, why doesn't your boss get a good old genetic test?"

Voorhies had described the need for the machine to work as spectacle. The politician had already gotten the test, but results, peer-reviewed papers, and genetic reports could be faked. No one believed them, but everyone responded to a bit of colour. While people like Louis wanted the science, Voorhies needed the show.

"Don't you have something to do?" Louis asked Gabe.

"What do you want to eat for lunch?"

"We just ate breakfast," Louis replied.

"That was three hours ago," Gabe said.

"Water," Emily said.

"I know where some is," Gabe said. The Cajun almost ran across the parking lot. On the other side of the street, he disappeared into a two-story building with a neon open sign that wasn't lit.

"He's just trying to help," Emily told Louis.

Louis tapped the monitor. "Where's your energy signature? I just know it has something to do with the machine."

"I thought it was me."

The exhaust from the machine cooled Emily. She shivered as if her skin was physically trying to emit energy into the air.

"I thought my lack of energy was the reason you didn't come by last night," Emily commented.

"I was on the phone."

Emily knew he was on the phone. He complained about it before they met Gabe. But did a phone call take all night?

"I thought you didn't want me to come," Louis said.

The machine's cooling fan continued to groan.

"I did."

"This isn't working," Louis said. He'd already got a new job back in Toronto. A medical company planned to explore techniques that oscillated fields to prevent cancer from forming in patients with a family history of the disease.

The cords swayed on the fence, and with the lack of activity, the screen shut down to save energy.

That afternoon, they set back up at the Evangeline oak. Lounging on a white concrete bench in the shade, Gabe sucked on a peppermint. Emily gravitated to the Cajun man. At least he talked to her, and he'd been right about the fried catfish he'd recommended earlier. Emily had eaten the entire plate. Her bloated stomach regretted it, but she'd order it again if she could.

Louis' energy detector whirred in the sun. In the heat, the sound irritated her.

"Have you ever tried cutting the fan?" Emily asked.

Louis draped the wires back out around the park.

"I'll take your boss's money, but I think he's wasting your time," Gabe told them. "These aren't even the trees Evangeline supposedly stood under. They're just for tourists."

As Emily's stomach processed her fish, it grumbled. During lunch, Emily outlined Voorhies's plan for re-election to Gabe. The Cajun flicked his hand, trying to shoo the squid and the whole idea away. The action reminded Emily of her brother. When he decided to leave, he swiped his hands in the air pushing away Emily's complaints. Emily had to stay home to take care of their mother. She could only assume the idea of babysitting her and their mother had repulsed him, so he made Emily do it. He'd even made her help him write his application essays—the ones that eventually got him the job in Toronto.

"At least there's shade," Gabe said.

Back home, Emily and her brother sat out in the sun without ever sweating, not like she was now. Here, even the squid's black body radiated heat.

"I want to know how that thing stays cool," Emily said.

"There's a fan," Louis replied.

She, of course, knew about the fan. Sitting in the sun, the droning noise never seemed to stop. Louis still reached in to prove his point, pulling a wire out of the squid. The whirring sound died somewhere behind the screen. As Louis leaned back to re-plug the fan, the monitor lit up. Rainbows of colours emanated from Emily's dot. Moreover, Emily's colours transmuted and joined a dark purple hue that hung around the periphery of the screen.

"The fan," Emily said. In the heat, the energy detector's fan hummed all day. The squid wasn't plugged into an outlet, so if the monitor worked without the fan on, the fan must be taking the majority of the power from an internal battery. "It's taking too much power."

Grabbing the wire, she yanked it out of his hand.

"What are you doing?" he asked.

The stream of her movement lit up the screen. Louis kissed the monitor.

Moments later, even Gabe circled the trees to watch his energy spiral around the park. Louis yanked out his phone and called Voorhies. "I fixed it," he said.

The fan had taken too much power from the squid. Louis had preprogrammed his energy into the machine back in Canada, so his readings used less power to display. That's why his showed up when Emily's and everyone else's didn't.

Maybe he did, but Emily kept repeating those words in her head. The wire she pulled from his hand left a friction burn on her palm. She even noticed a similar mark on his hand, but he ignored it. By the end of the day, Louis had not only obtained enough data to guarantee a successful campaign rally for Voorhies, but had gathered enough hard evidence to showcase his discovery for the rest of his scientific career.

Overjoyed, Voorhies sent Emily a ticket for a teleport to wherever she wanted to go. That night, when Louis came to her motel door with his own teleport pass in hand, Emily slammed that door in his face. The next day, she tore up her ticket and hitchhiked by herself.

5

THE NIGHT LIBRARIAN BY HELEN POWER

The words were scrawled in block letters on the sleek metal washroom stall door. "HAVE A NICE DAY", followed by a drooping smiley face. I rolled my eyes at the overly-polite graffiti. "Only in Canada," I muttered as I inspected the ink. It looked permanent.

All the history books said that Canadians were significantly friendlier than those from other countries. I could never know for sure because all the other countries—and the people living in them—were long gone. Everything was destroyed by the Great Cataclysm of 2067. But I had read a lot of books written before the world ended, and I knew that if I had been working in a library anywhere else, the vandalism would have been a lot less well-mannered.

I reached into the janitor's toolkit and retrieved the E-raser, a small, handheld device that could theoretically erase "everything". I supposed I would be putting it to the test. As a librarian, cleaning the washrooms went far beyond my job description, but the night janitor hadn't shown up, so I was the only person working that night. Surprisingly, the graffiti came off easily. The E-raser sliced through the ink with exact and startling precision.

Finished with my menial task, I returned the janitor's toolbox to the nearest utility closet. I hurried down the aisles of bookcases, eager to get out of the basement level. Every shelf was overflowing with boxes of microfilm that we *still* hadn't earned the funding to digitize. A wealth of historical information trapped in an obsolete format. I stepped into the elevator-pod. With a quiet whir, it deposited me on the ground floor. I exited and strode down the empty halls, the sound of my heels clacking against polished marble echoing across the high ceilings. The National Library—the nation's *only* library—was designed by Clara DuFond, New Canada's most preeminent architect of the twenty-first century, who had evolved the Beaux-Arts style of architecture to incorporate contemporary technology.

I settled into my chair at the circulation desk and slipped on a pair of well-worn protective gloves. I opened the antique book I was reading, careful not to crack the spine. This was the world's last copy of "The Handmaid's Tale" by Margaret Atwood, and I would *not* be responsible for damaging such a valuable and rare piece of Canadian literature.

My name was Charlotte Babineaux, and I was the night librarian at The National Library. It was my responsibility to collect, preserve, share, and protect information from before —and after—the Great Cataclysm of 2067. This included the plethora of information that was once on the internet, which was now stored in the sleek servers situated in the lower levels of the building. The Library housed everything—from priceless art to the government's most top-secret reports and documents. These mostly comprised of the Architects' blueprints for our country, and the climate scientists' annual environmental scans, all of which were stored in a highly secure vault in the basement. Not even I had access to it.

When I graduated from the University with a degree in Library and Information Science, I was surprised to discover that in order to be a Librarian, I also had to undergo vigorous physical training so I could protect the Library's secrets. I was instructed in Karate, Tae Kwon Do, and meditation—the latter was more for my nerves than anything else.

In addition to the government's most well-guarded secrets, the Library was home to a great number of print books. Because not everything could be saved, preference had been given to Canadian Literature. I had been slowly working my way through the classics on these cold, desolate winter nights. While the Library was technically open twenty-four hours a day, I rarely saw patrons who were interested in research or finding their next favourite read during the dead of the night. I used to work with another librarian, but due to cutbacks, I had to hold down the fort alone from eleven to seven, when most of New Canada was tucked away in their warm beds. I didn't mind the solitude since it gave me the opportunity to brush up on old-Canadian literature.

An alert sounded from my *Appel*, a communications device that was small enough to fit in the palm of my hand, but loud enough to echo across the loud, empty halls. Sighing, I glanced over at its screen. It was a news alert. But not just any kind of news alert. It was a *crime* news alert. That couldn't be right.

"*Appel*, read the headline," I commanded.

"Woman Found Murdered with Half-Digested Poutine in Her Stomach."

A chill crept down my spine. Statistically, there was an average of three murders a year in New Canada. We'd already reached two, and it was only February. A few weeks earlier, Dr. Jia Chen had been run over by a hijacked Zamboni. I would never look at a Zamboni the same way again.

"*Appel*, show me the article." My voice shook slightly.

Former burlesque dancer and current janitor at The National Library, Lisette Bouchard, found dead on the corner of Wellington and Elgin at 11 PM today.

Guilt washed over me. I'd been wishing her dead as I scrubbed the toilets, and she hadn't shown up to work because she already *was* dead.

An autopsy scan has revealed that the 42-year-old was shot in the head point blank. Partially digested poutine from Trudeau's Treats *was detected in her digestive tract, indicating that she consumed it merely 30 minutes before her death. Detective Lyons assured the* Canadian Sun *that "there's no cause for alarm" and that this is "likely a one-time crime", before returning to his box of Timbits.*

The article didn't have enough information. How was Lisette shot? There were hardly any *pistolets* in New Canada. All *pistolets* were registered and a ballistics scan would have quickly identified the killer. Why wasn't that information included in the news alert? And usually when there was a murder in New Canada the prime minister made a statement. Although, Prime Minister Marybeth Warren hadn't been well lately. She was pushing ninety and currently up for her 9th term. She'd won the last eight elections by a landslide, and had led New Canada into peaceful times for thirty-two years. But this past election she'd had a real contender, Arthur Crouch of the Freedom Party. Crouch had gained popularity with the younger crowd by appealing to their distrust of science.

I glanced around, paranoia rising with all the little hairs on my arms. The Library was quiet. *Too* quiet. I turned to the console.

"Show me the access log," I ordered.

The Library was empty and had been for the two hours since I'd started my shift at eleven. I tapped my fingers on the cold stone of the desk as I thought this over. Protocol indicated that in the case of emergency, I must lock up for the night. Of course, the protocols were written for when there was an accidental fire or attempted robbery, not a possibly-unrelated murder. But my gut told me this was bad news.

Following the established protocol in the case of an emergency, I made a quick sweep of every floor to make sure the Library was empty. The Library required everyone to scan their New Canadian Citizenship (NCC) chip—embedded in their right wrist—at the front door to be granted entrance, so I wasn't surprised to find that there were no library patrons or potential murderers in the stacks. As I left, I locked the big gated door behind me. It required a physical key, my handprint, *and* a retinal scan to be unlocked. The nation's secrets would be safe for the night, even though the Library hadn't technically closed in over two years, not since the year the New Canada Day celebratory fireworks had damaged the country's weather simulation monitors. I hoped I wasn't overreacting about the murder of the janitor, or else I would be in for an earful from the day librarian when he showed up for his shift at seven and I wasn't here.

On the street, a cold gust of wind rustled my auburn curls, and I hastily put up my hood. I glanced up at the moonless sky. Artificial stars winked down at me.

A hundred years ago, the Architects of the country had assembled to build a safe haven for its citizens. They had wisely anticipated the Great Cataclysm of 2067. The US had finally acknowledged that climate change existed, and they were determined to do something about it. Rather than cutting down on fossil fuel emissions or funding renewable energy research, they had created a device, a large solar-powered machine that would remove the greenhouse gases from the atmosphere. Climate scientists had warned that the atmosphere needed *some* carbon dioxide to sustain life, but of course, the American president hadn't listened to them. The climatologists, tired of being ignored, moved north to Canada where they collaborated with the Architects to create a safe haven.

Our self-sustaining country was based on designs already created by Swedish scientists. Built on northern Ontario farmlands, it was almost three thousand square kilometres in area and completely self-contained. Its contents were entirely cut-off from the outside world and any potential toxins, but its domed roof was high enough to mimic the real sky. Inside, a state-of-the-art city was built. Mirroring downtown Ottawa, it even had its own Rideau Canal and Parliament Buildings.

Historical photographs of the outside of the country always reminded me of a beaver dam—at least—photographs I'd seen of beaver dams. I'd never seen a beaver outside of New Canada's only zoo, Noah's Ark. New Canada looked like it had been patched together haphazardly, which might have been because the Architects had so little time to have it built. The Swedish design was much sleeker looking. I always wondered if Sweden had gotten their new country built in time. Once Canada's safe haven was built, inhabitants were selected by highly-rigged lottery, and they immediately moved in. Not long after this transfer, the Great Cataclysm occurred, and all of the rest of Canada —and every other country in the world—was lost forever. Now named New Canada, this safe haven was the only thing protecting humanity from extinction.

There were police cars and bright yellow tape a few blocks away. The crime scene looked abandoned. The detectives were probably still at Tim Hortons—fueling up on much-needed coffee and donuts. The country had only one library, but there were nineteen Tim Hortons—and they were looking to expand further. Sighing, I turned and headed toward home.

I stuffed my hands into my pockets and traipsed through the two-foot-high snow. I wasn't sure why the Architects had deemed it necessary to have the weather simulators imitate all four seasons. I supposed that they thought it would feel more like home to the citizens. I was fourth generation New Canadian, and I personally could do without these harsh New Canadian winters.

I scanned my NCC chip to get into my condominium. My heart skipped a beat as I approached my front door. It was ajar.

Fists at the ready, I kicked the door open. The overhead lights were already activated, revealing an empty foyer. Recognizing my NCC chip, the front door automatically closed and locked behind me. I stormed through the apartment. Surprise was my best weapon.

I found him in the study. A tall, slender man wearing an over-sized black toque pulled down over his eyebrows was rummaging around in my desk drawer. Too late, I realized that that was where I kept my *pistolet*. But he didn't pull it out. Instead, he charged at me, knocking me against the wall. My head slammed against the plaster. I shook away the dizziness as something cold and wet touched my left hand. Not sure what was happening, I curled the fingers on my other hand into a fist and I swung around, punching the intruder squarely in the jaw. Dazed, he stumbled backward. Something hit me from behind, knocking me to the ground.

Toque had a partner. I spun around, sizing him up. The second man was shorter but more muscular. He grinned at me, revealing a missing front tooth. He was about to lose more. I dropped to the ground and swept the floor with my feet, and Hockey Teeth dropped like a sack of potatoes. Toque came up behind me and shoved me against the desk. He flipped me over and held something over my eyes. Bright red light blinded me. I flipped him over my head and spun around. Hockey Teeth was already back on his feet.

"You two loonies are in for a world of hurt," I said, swaying slightly.

Toque and Hockey Teeth exchanged a look, then dashed toward the window. They catapulted out into the night.

I blinked. I knew I looked frightening with my crisp chignon and horn-rimmed glasses, but it shouldn't have been *that* easy.

I hurried to the desk and yanked open the drawer that Toque had been searching. My *pistolet* was still there. Why hadn't he used it on me?

Pounding erupted at the front door.

"RCMP! OPEN UP!"

That was the fastest response time I'd ever seen from the Mounties.

"We know it was your *pistolet* that was used to kill the janitor!" one voice called out.

"Shut up! Don't tell her that!" another said.

Ice cold fear coursed through my veins as I stared down at the desk drawer. Toque hadn't been looking for my *pistolet*. He'd been returning it.

The pounding on the front door continued.

"We know you're in there, Charlotte Babineaux! Your NCC chip was used to lock your door less than five minutes ago!"

"Shut *up!*"

This wasn't a coincidence. Those men had killed Lisette, framing me. When they found out that she didn't have a key or biometric access to the Library, they came after me.

The cold feeling on my hand. The bright light that had been pointed into my eye. Those were for the palm print and retinal scans. I groped around in my pockets, but my key was missing. They must have been lifted during the fight without my noticing.

The realization of what was happening slowly sank in, and I leaned heavily against the wall. These criminals had access to the National Library and its secrets.

I didn't have time to explain this to the Mounties. I didn't have time to hope that they would listen. I retrieved my spare key for the Library from my safe, which was concealed by a print of Tom Tomson's *The Jack Pine*. I jumped at the splintering crash of the Mounties breaking down my front door. I dove toward the window and escaped the same way as the intruders.

I raced through the snow, cursing the ineptitude of the snow plows and the idiocy of the existence of weather simulators. A storm was picking up, something that wasn't predicted by the meteorologists. One would think that the weather man would be accurate when the weather was simulated.

By the time I reached the Library, I was soaked through to the skin, and I couldn't tell if I was shivering or sweating. The Library looked abandoned. Maybe I'd made it here first.

I unlocked the library with the spare key and my biometrics scans. I slipped through the door and closed it firmly behind me, reactivating lockdown.

I turned and peered around the large, imposing entrance hall. The only illumination came from the glowing red emergency lights. I ventured a few steps deeper into the Library. I couldn't know how much time I had before the intruders arrived.

What was I doing? I couldn't defend the Library by myself. I needed to tell the police. I needed to tell the Prime Minister.

I took out my *Appel* and called the direct line to Prime Minister Warren.

Ring. Ring. Ring.

I cocked my head, ripping the *Appel* away from my ear. The ringing was coming *from inside the Library.*

Ring. Ring. Ri--.

I pushed forward, following the sound until it cut off abruptly. The Library was large and drafty and sounds travelled far among its vast, echoic halls. The sound could have come from anywhere.

The Vault.

I knew without a doubt that Warren's life was in jeopardy. I slipped into the stairwell and descended into the bowels of the Library. I exited onto the sub-level where had I scrubbed graffiti earlier that night. It felt like a lifetime ago that I had been down here when in reality it had been merely hours.

At that thought, I ducked into the utility closet to retrieve something. I hoped to God that I wouldn't have to use it.

Creeping down the aisles, past the long-abandoned microfilm, I was grateful that the automatic lights were deactivated when the building was on lockdown.

Hushed voices sounded up ahead. Toque and Hockey Teeth stood in the narrow space in front of the vault. A third man accompanied them. I recognized him instantly.

I couldn't contain my gasp. Three pairs of eyes shot toward me. I stumbled backward, clawing for my *pistolet*, but I wasn't fast enough.

Toque was suddenly upon me. In two swift moves, he grabbed my arm and my *pistolet*, tossing it to the side and dragging me toward the others.

Arthur Crouch, the leader of the Freedom Party, gazed down at me with shrewd green eyes that were drawn together by wiry eyebrows. "The night librarian?" he asked Toque.

"She's been framed. We can't kill her," Hockey Teeth said. "At least, not yet."

"You can't get into the vault." I sounded smug. "You need..." Hockey Teeth's toothless grin stopped me mid-sentence.

Only the prime minister could get into that vault. But her *Appel* was down here. Which meant...

Arthur Crouch's lips spread into a flat smile. He reached behind a bookshelf and retrieved a limp and barely conscious Marybeth Warren. He positioned her head in front of the retinal scanner. The light turned green.

"Prime Minister, are you all right?" I tried to move toward her, but Toque twisted my arm painfully.

Warren didn't respond, didn't react as Crouch placed her hand on the palm reader.

The second light turned green.

That just left the password.

Crouch smiled at me as he pulled out his *Appel* and tapped a button. "Maple syrup." Warren's voice was clear but highly distraught.

The third light flashed green, and the vault door silently

slid open. Crouch dropped Warren to the ground, where she crumpled in a heap.

"Why—what are you doing? What are you looking for?" I finally found the words to speak.

Crouch smiled at me, condescendingly. "Poor child. You don't even realize you're a prisoner here."

I blinked at him.

"New Canada. It's a prison," he said.

Realization dawned on me. He was spouting the same lies he told his followers. The same words he brought with him on the campaign trail. A campaign he lost.

"It's not a prison. It's a *haven*."

Crouch laughed, a high-pitched sound that grated my ears and sent a shiver down my spine. "A *haven*? Don't you realize that science is a lie? It's safe on the outside! I'm here to prove that."

The Architects' blueprints. The roadmap they used to build this safe haven was housed within this vault. Everything was in those documents, from the mechanics behind the weather simulator to the secret backdoor. A backdoor which, if opened, would bring down the entire country, killing everyone in it.

I shook my head furiously. "Haven't you read the environmental scans? The outside is toxic! It cannot sustain life!"

Crouch laughed again, his eyes crazed. "It's a conspiracy. I consulted many of my own scientists, and I found one that says it's safe on the outside."

"*One*?" I spat.

Crouch entered the vault, approaching the blueprints, which were displayed prominently on a glass table in the centre of the room. The walls were lined with shelves, piled high with climate science reports. The vault held information so valuable that it couldn't be digitized, for fear it would get into the wrong hands. Hands that were now inching toward it.

As a librarian, it was my responsibility to collect, preserve, and share information. But, as a librarian of the twenty-second century, it was also my duty to protect that information. To protect the truth. No matter the cost.

I dropped to the ground, kicking Toque in the shin, and sending a swift uppercut to his jaw. He went out like a light.

Crouch pulled out a *pistolet* and pointed it at my head. He made it clear—me or the blueprints. But if he got access to the blueprints, that would mean the fall of New Canada.

I would die either way.

I reached into my pocket and pulled out the item I'd retrieved earlier. The E-raser. Without hesitation, I pointed it at the blueprints. The blue ink sliced away into nothingness until the pages were blank. Light smoke curled from the tip of the laser.

Crouch howled, "What have you done?" Wild with rage, he *pistolet*-butted me and I slammed into a shelf. A folder toppled to the ground, where it flipped open and loose pages scattered like leaves in the wind.

Three armed Mounties appeared in the doorway. Crouch's anger seemed to drain out of him like a sieve. He didn't say another word as he was zip-tied and led away.

"You've done your country a great service here, today." Prime Minister Warren had not only regained consciousness, but she was also standing—albeit she was leaning heavily against the nearest shelf.

I didn't look at her. My eyes were glued to the climate science report I had knocked to the ground. The name on the report was familiar: Dr. Jia Chen. Heart in my throat, I skimmed the report's executive summary.

I looked up to discover Warren was watching me closely. "I really wish you hadn't read that."

Was it true? Was it possible that Crouch *wasn't* lying, or insane? I opened my mouth to speak, but Warren cut me off.

"New Canada is safe from the outside world. Whether the threat is environmental or...otherwise is irrelevant."

My entire body was tense, but I managed to nod. "I understand."

Warren smiled at me, but the warmth didn't quite reach her eyes. We exited the vault, its door sliding shut behind us.

"Your silence is utterly critical for peace in New Canada," Warren continued.

"I understand," I repeated.

I did understand. I had read enough classic dystopian fiction to understand perfectly well what was going on. Everything I knew about this world was from the history books stored here in the Library. But books were written by people, and information could easily be manipulated.

I walked out into the artificial night, the Mounties stepping aside to let me pass. I was a hero in their eyes. Shivering, I gazed up at the clear sky. There was no sign of the storm that had ravaged the night.

I had caught a glimpse of the blueprints before they had been destroyed forever. I knew the location of the door to the outside world. I approached the street, but I didn't turn toward home. Instead, I went in the opposite direction.

As a librarian, it was my responsibility to collect, preserve, and protect information. But as a librarian of the twenty-second century, it was also my duty to share information. To share the truth. No matter the cost.

6
CARBON CONCERNS BY RYAN TOXOPEUS

Monique stood so close to the transparent, shimmering wall that its tingling energy made the fine hairs on her arms stand up on end under her winter coat. The cold turned her breath into even clouds of moisture, but none of it crossed the barrier.

While it was called a "wall," it bore no resemblance to the brick and mortar types that still made up so many Canadian homes. No, the ingenuity of Canadian scientists had struck once more, and none too soon.

Canada's long history of scientific achievements, from the Avro Arrow to the Canadarm, was crowned by the latest invention. The project had been named "wall"—a play on the tyrant king Trump's southern border wall—by its inventor, Christi Favreau-Smith. She was a professor of physics at McGill University and was brilliant by anyone's standards, and perhaps doubly so by those of Monique, who cherished her partner more than anyone else in the world.

Monique had been bullied through her formative years over her attraction to other women. "Zero tolerance" for bullying had sounded nice in theory, but when held up to scrutiny had meant less than nothing. Teachers and principals would reprimand the bullies, but it just happened again and again, until Monique didn't even bother reporting it anymore. It wasn't until she entered university, with Christi's help, that Monique had battled her depression to finally create her own world-changing invention.

While fires raged across the continental Broken States of America, fueled by nuclear and conventional weapons, that all-consuming conflagration remained south of the wall. The low-cost, solar-powered emitters, spaced at regular intervals along Canada's entire border, provided practical protection against all of Trump's weapons, and those of his enemies who had bombarded much of both coasts into ruin.

Perhaps it wasn't a simple coincidence that the attacks had been launched immediately after Canada had powered up the wall. No doubt even America's fiercest opponents had second-guessed any attack on the old USA when Canada could have been rocked by collateral damage. With most of the Canadian population living near the border, Canada could have been obliterated along with the USA in any large scale attacks. Little would have stirred the ire of the world faster than the peacekeeping nation falling along with its southern neighbour.

Whatever the motivation, North Korea's nuclear weapons had been far more advanced than anyone had given them credit for. With the USA already broken by its latest civil war, it hadn't taken much to further destabilize and destroy the country.

With puppet Trump at the helm of the white supremacist forces, who had consolidated their power in the south before the new civil war, Putin had launched his own offensive against Europe. Ukraine had already lost strategic defensive positions in the east and had offered no meaningful resistance to the invading forces. Coordinated nuclear strikes using shipping cargo containers in Shanghai's harbour and delivery trucks in Beijing had crippled the Chinese. The once-Allied forces had become the Axis, and in an unlikely turn of events, Kim Jong-un had become a hero of the resistance, rallying China's survivors to defend the world.

Well, the rest of the world, Monique thought, while watching the wildfires obliterate the southern forests. Estimates of the war's impact on the environment were catastrophic. With fires raging unchecked, the atmosphere might never recover.

Or so they thought.

Monique performed a final series of checks on her nanobot army. Communications were good. Systems checked normal. It was time to put the little gals to work.

There was always a sense of trepidation when bringing laboratory-tested hardware into the field. But time was running out. Water levels had already taken out large portions of coastal cities, from Metro Vancouver to Charlottetown's harbourfront. In fact, scientists had issued warnings about a possible runaway climate-change event, with Earth turning into the next Venus. Christi had assured her that the bots were ready.

Thousands of tiny engines kicked to life, and Monique entered the details of the bots' first foray into her tablet. In an instant, they were gone. The hum dissipated into smaller clusters of whining, and then to nothing as the nanobots scattered through the air. The tablet told her that some of the bots had lifted high into the atmosphere to travel over the wall and begin their work in the polluted skies over the Broken States of America. Others started working on the carbon dioxide on the Canadian side of the wall. The rest remained on the ground, awaiting the fruits of the labours of the airborne nanobots.

Powered by the sun, the technology could feasibly reverse the effects of carbon in the atmosphere. Had it been powered by traditional fuels, it would have created as much carbon dioxide as it destroyed.

The control screen flashed a green light, and Monique swore she could almost feel the carbon atoms peppering her. The bots cleaved them off the carbon dioxide molecules and worked to bind the carbon atoms together, fusing them into solid, inert chunks. But the molecules were so tiny, she had been told any sense of being bombarded by invisible bits of carbon was purely psychological. Her program ensured none of the nanobots would enter a person's airways, but even so, she couldn't help but feel like they were entering her mouth and lungs with every breath.

With the bots away, she had time to think before she would need to check on their status again. Was Christi all right, back in Montreal? Would the two of them really ever be happy together? Already there were rumblings that the "end times" were upon them. Firebrand preachers blamed liberal views of tolerance toward the LGBTQQICAPF2K+ community for the destruction across the globe. Hatred for minorities was breaking apart communities. While Canada had been an early adopter of solidarity, she feared it was going down the path that had destroyed its southern neighbour.

Monique lost track of time as her mind spiralled into darkness.

An hour later, her tablet beeped at her. The display showed the nanobots continued to work flawlessly. On the ground, a second wave of bots used the carbon-carbon bonded pairs to fashion carbon nanotubes, which they turned into tiny solar panels and more nanobots. They had nearly doubled their numbers and showed no sign of slowing. In fact, the coding for the nanobots ensured they would continue to replicate and work until the atmospheric carbon was brought back down to 250 parts per million, a level widely deemed as safe.

It was working. Monique trembled with the realization that this research could save the world. Canada could survive and share the technology with allies, creating impenetrable borders and clean air for everyone...

And continue to deal with petty politics and war another day. What was she saving? It was a debate she'd had with Christi many times, and here she was on the brink of saving humanity one more time. Would they learn from past mistakes, or were they doomed to continue finding new and inventive ways of destroying themselves? She had never totally shaken her belief that humans were manipulative and violent by nature.

Already she could envision someone finding a way to weaponize her nanobots, using them to perhaps cleave atoms off molecules in the human brain, or other organs. Undetected, they could wipe out or mutate targets, and then how would she feel? It certainly wasn't unprecedented for a peaceful technology to be used for war. Not that she would ever dare compare her work to Einstein's, but she couldn't shake the knowledge that his work on atomic energy had been twisted to create bombs.

In her youth, Monique would have been proud to carry on Canada's longstanding tradition of keeping peace around the world, but the fact that humanity continued to need peacekeepers bothered her. Her father—her protector—had died in Afghanistan, on the other side of the world, for nothing. In his absence, she had needed to defend herself—and Christi—from bigots and homophobes. And what had they gained invading that godforsaken land? Opium, fueling an opioid addiction epidemic across the western world. Drug companies raked in profits while people died of their addictions. No, her father hadn't died for nothing. He had died to ensure corporate overlords made a profit, whether it was from weapons or drug sales. She felt her pulse quickening with her mounting anger.

Staring at her screen, she watched the progress bar glow green as a thousand more nanobots came online. She opened the program and found the lines of code she wanted already highlighted, waiting for her to take action.

Copying the code, she pasted it into a second block. She replaced the variable "carbon dioxide" with "copper" and stared at the screen a while longer. Each second that ticked by, more nanobots joined the swarm. She added another block of code, defining that there was a fifty percent chance that a new nanobot would cleave carbon dioxide and a fifty percent chance that it would cleave copper. A last check confirmed in her mind that half of the nanobots would continue to build themselves with carbon, while the other half worked toward her vision of the future.

She tucked the code away and opened her messaging application, which automatically added Christi as the recipient. Christi's smiling face with those cute dimples gazed at her. It was almost enough to shake her resolve.

"It worked. I'm sorry," Monique wrote, even though she wasn't. This was for the best. She sent the message and closed the messaging application. A tap on the screen brought up the window with the updated code again.

She saved the code and ran it. A second later the copper wires in the tablet were severed. Canada had phased out the penny because the copper was more valuable in electronics because of its high conductivity and malleability. It was modern society's greatest vulnerability.

Monique looked up as the copper connections in the wall emitters failed, and the barrier dropped.

Fire swept across the border.

May it be a better world for whatever species came next.

7

HER LAST WALK BY PAUL WILLIAMS

Originally Published in *Dark Helix Ezine*,
Issue #3, Spring 2019

The termination email arrived at 09:01 but Geraldine didn't see it until an hour later when her game of bingo finished. Every day she joined players around the world, listening to excited voices shouting and sometimes calling out herself to claim a win. She didn't know their real names or what they looked like as she disabled the camera. Sometimes she imagined them as elderly, from the generation after hers. The kind of people who used to play at the King's Bingo Club, across the road. Where her late husband met her replacement. Six years ago, the bulldozers knocked it down and erected a shopping mall to block her view. When she looked across the gleaming white walls she felt that she lived in a morgue. Or on Death Row. Toronto was full of white walls now. When it snowed you couldn't see the city.

At the end of the game, she read all the emails, whilst waiting for the kettle to boil. She missed real coffee. The granules tasted worse than usual, because she left the kettle standing whilst she read and reread to be sure that she understood. Sometimes she had to magnify the screen. Her glasses were twenty-one years old. She never responded to annual reminders from the optician.

The termination email came from an address that she didn't recognize but it had bypassed the junk filter so had to be official. *Geraldine Mitchell*, it began. No prefix. *You are approaching the eightieth anniversary of your birth.* A birthday. Once she celebrated but now dates had no meaning. *In accordance with the Canadian Care of Senior Citizens Act (2056) and the Protection of the Public Purse Act (2057), the following day, 10 January, is scheduled for your termination. You will be collected from your residential address at 09:00. There will be no charge for transportation. If you have a life insurance policy, you may wish to commence any claim now to prevent delays.*

Thank you for your assistance in this matter and we hope that you enjoyed your life.

It was not signed. Sighing she sat down and filed a life insurance claim, eventually finding a provider who didn't require a mandatory phone number. Then she hobbled to the window, pushed it open, and looked across at the silent mall wondering what it was like to live in the modern world.

The next day after Bingo and coffee, she wrote a will specifying a charity to receive the considerable surplus in her bank account following deduction of funeral expenses. Then she googled the charity to check that it still existed. On the third day, she posted a message on her Facebook accounts, saying goodbye. She had 1982 friends, but most were older and already dead. Eight of the survivors liked her activity but she only recognized one of the names. Nobody commented or replied. She checked every hour, in between gazes through the window. Once she suffered from the illusion that people cared. It went away with her husband's betrayal, but she still expected a response to her existence.

On the fourth day, a robot delivered her weekly groceries. Always the same. Always immaculate and tasteless. She yearned for traditional fish and chips with the grease and oil that home cooking couldn't replicate. She stacked the supplies neatly in their allocated space in the fridge, then emailed to cancel future deliveries. The supermarket immediately sent back their regret, unsigned, along with a feedback questionnaire and a discount voucher for future use.

On the fifth day, she read blogs written by people before their termination. Canada adopted the legislation after the United States and the United Kingdom and most of the better blogs were from citizens who died in those countries. They all advised going outside on the day before. Geraldine normally ignored advice, after everyone told her she would be fine and then ignored her when she wasn't, but the blogs got her thinking more strongly about life in the city that had once been a street. She had to find out. One last adventure.

On the sixth day, after bingo, she put on a coat and hat for the first time in twenty years. The coat was a bit big, but the hat still fitted. The corridor outside was the same, except for a relatively new carpet. The anonymous neighbours now had a Do Not Disturb sign on their door. She never bothered with signs, just didn't answer the door to anyone apart from the delivery robot. She hit the lift button and waited, realizing that she had forgotten to cancel her bingo subscription. Would her gaming friends miss her or quickly find a replacement? Like her husband did.

The door opened onto a corridor with the same carpet as the one above. She walked through the revolving exit and onto the street. The pavements were narrower than she remembered, allowing for an overtaking lane. They were free from ice, which was a blessing.

Cars, all small and without drivers, passed noiselessly. No pedestrians. She gazed at the white stilts holding the mall upright and found a lift, touch sensitive, to enter. The air inside felt just as stale. She passed dozens of small shops, mostly staffed by robots. Few had customers. People with despondent faces queued at either the jobcentre or the medical centre. Some might be waiting for voluntary termination. It felt no different to her apartment. Part of the world but not in it. Tomorrow she would learn if there was somewhere better.

She saw the logo of the supermarket and entered, seeking a last coffee. Robots moved silently around her, even the trolleys were quiet, collecting groceries to deliver. It was a shop built for people, but people no longer shopped. She found the coffee aisle with bags of identical looking beans but no café. Avoiding the uniformed security robot who looked exactly like she imagined a termination robot to look, she returned to the corridor, and studied a map on the wall, activated by touch. Her arthritic fingers slowly traced a path to the word she wanted to see. CAFÉ. On the bottom floor, five escalators down, she discovered a food court. Some of the shops had familiar signs and bored human staff. She heard voices and made her way towards them.

Four old women sat around a table with cups of coffee and biscuit. She made her way to a quieter corner but they all stared at her.

"Gerry," said one.

It was her turn to stare. The voice sounded familiar. The speaker's face was hidden by glasses like hers. She squinted. "Hilda," she said.

Hilda smiled. "Haven't seen you since the funeral."

"But you're older than me. How can you still be alive?'

The women all laughed. "You got the email, didn't you?" said Hilda. "I saw it on Facebook, thought about messaging you but didn't know if you'd appreciate that."

Geraldine had forgotten that Hilda was one of her Facebook friends. She didn't know the other women but perhaps they had been there at one of the coffee sessions. It started as a social for the women whose husbands were addicted to Bingo. Then Hilda crossed the line, after her partner's death. Started going to Bingo, trying to steal someone else's partner. Some people couldn't live alone. Had to have company.

Geraldine was different. She managed twenty years on her own and she wasn't going to have her last day ruined. "I can't stay," she said. The words sounded hollow. One of the other women pulled a chair across and gestured for her to sit down.

"Alive or here?" asked Hilda.

"No choice about dying."

"It's not compulsory. The politicians realized that one day it might be them or their loved ones, so they wrote an exception clause."

"What exception?"

"Don't answer the door. Don't let the robot in. Not authorized to force entry." Hilda signalled to a waitress. "Get this lady a drink and then we'll take her shopping. You wore that hat and coat to the funeral. Surprised it still fits."

Geraldine removed her coat, remembering the crowd of mourners and then the reading of the will. Hilda received a legacy. Nobody ever explained why, but everybody knew. Some of them had made excuses when he was off with her. She knew that she couldn't trust them again and was better off on her own. Living the remainder of her life in peace. Spending the legacy that came to her on her husband's favourite game. Proving that she was better than him to erase the memories.

"Why don't the survivors blog," she said. "If it's true."

"They're scared," said Hilda. "Scared that the government will find them and bring in rules to cancel their bank accounts or their pensions. We live out of sight, it's easy now when the only contact you may need is with a doctor. And frankly, if you reach the point where you want more than an automated diagnosis, you're ready to die."

The waitress placed a coffee in front of Geraldine who finally sat. "We're here every day at nine-thirty," said Hilda. "Except the second Thursday of the month when we have fish and chips. You're welcome to join us. Look like you need some friends."

"Every day," she repeated.

"It started when we worried about the robots coming back. What if we left the door open accidentally or a visitor did. Plus, our apartments started to feel like death row. I guess we weren't meant to live alone."

"Or die," said Geraldine.

Hilda passed her a biscuit. "That terrified me for years," she said. "I watched Barry die. Didn't want to end up like him but one day it's got to happen."

"I watched someone die too," she said.

Hilda nodded. "I felt guilty about that legacy. He told me a month before, said I was the best bingo partner ever. I wasn't that great, just lucky, and don't play now. Come to the same place but prefer coffee. Are you going to tell us why you became a recluse?"

Geraldine left the mall at 13:10 and made her way home, not recognizing her building at first. There was a reminder email about the termination appointment in her inbox. She cancelled her bingo subscription and reread her will then deleted it.

At 08:45 the following morning, 9 January, she put on her new hat and coat and hung her new other new purchase on the door. At 09:01 she passed a robot in the corridor and watched it approach her door. Ignoring the "Do Not Disturb" sign it knocked loudly with its metal hand. Nobody answered. The robot waited a few minutes then trundled back past her and into the lift. She let it descend before pressing the button.

8

MOTHER OF THE CARIBOU BY CHRISTINE RAINS

Qaaynak shielded her eyes from the bright light and squinted to see the hunt in the distance. The faint shapes of wolves creeping toward an old caribou shimmered in the snowy wind. She gripped her lance tighter. All it would take was one jolt from it and the wolves would flee.

"Sit with me. I will tell you the tale of how the caribou came to be." Her grandfather patted the bench beside him.

She couldn't turn her eyes away. Didn't want to. Her heart beat hard in her chest. Was the animal crying? No doubt it was frightened. Death did not have to be so brutal.

Communities in the south didn't let their herds grow old. They genetically engineered all the animals to be in prime condition and put the beasts to sleep before the ravages of age took a hold of them. It was a gentler way of life.

"Granddaughter, hear me."

Qaaynak sighed. Her shoulders slumped, and she turned before the wolves could pounce upon their prey. "Why must there be wolves, Grandfather? The land is not what it once was, hardy and pristine. If we are to tend the caribou, we can do so with a more humane rule."

"There is nothing humane about nature, child. The Earth knows what she's about no matter how we try to control her. We should follow her lead rather than try to put her in chains."

She watched him adjust his ocular implant even as he kept his gaze upon the hunt. He'd celebrated his ninety-first birthday the previous month and still moved like a young man with his cybernetics. He could not speak to her about letting nature lead the way.

"You do not agree," he stated.

Leaning forward with one hand on her knee, she kicked at the snow that had never seen the sky. Instead, it had descended from the machines spaced between the lights on the ceiling. "It's not that. Things are different now. The old ways cannot mesh with the new ways. I only want our community to thrive."

"But we do. We do not lack for anything. Wind powers our home, robots work the greenhouses and mine minerals for our printers to build tools and materials. Our habitats are programmed to sustain themselves." Her grandfather gestured to the snowy scape before them. "All we must do is oversee them. What more do we need?"

The old folks never understand. Not only did she want their home beneath the melted tundra to thrive, but she wanted it to go beyond expectations. To learn, to grow, to find a way to clean the Earth's polluted surface and reclaim it again. So that she herself could reclaim a part of herself that felt lost. No matter that she was born in the dome, she yearned to break free of it.

Her grandfather would have everything remain the same forever, but so much had changed their little lonely corner of northern Canada already. With the permafrost gone, oil spills soaked into the ground as if it were a sponge. Animals and plants suffered as the water slowly poisoned them. The winds which once blew cold and sharp now came hot and angry with storms like the land had never seen before.

"Did you want to hear my tale now?"

No. She didn't. She should have let Aujaq come out with their grandfather today. At seven, he was younger than her by five years, but he liked listening to the old stories as much as he liked those quest games he played on the interlink.

Be respectful. She told herself.

Qaaynak could at least manage that. "If you want, Grandfather."

The wolves had brought down their meal. Fast and efficient, there was very little struggle. Now they feasted, and her stomach churned.

He took in a deep breath and slowly released it. The wind whisked away his misty exhale. "When Raven made Man, he found him to be lonely. So he created a companion called Woman. For some time, they were happy. The Man would go away for long periods to fish, and soon, the Woman grew lonely.

"She dug a deep hole into the ground, and that hole bore countless caribou. When she deemed there was enough for the whole world, she covered the hole. Man found the beasts good for food and hunted them, but when one animal fell ill, the disease spread to many others in the herd. Man alone could not stop it.

"So Woman opened the hole again and out came the wolves. The wolves hunted the old and sick. From the caribou, the pack grew strong. And from the wolves, the herd grew strong. The wolves and the caribou need one another."

Qaaynak grasped the harmony of their existence, and it

made her smile a little. It was simple, and it still could be, but in a different way. A way that flowed with their changed land. She would find that path, one where humans lived in unity with nature instead of forcing the environment to adapt to them.

"And one day, if we're all very lucky," her grandfather turned to face her and placed a hand on her hooded head. "You will be the woman who opens our hole in the ground and releases the caribou back into the world."

Yes, a new way, back on the surface, where they would not only thrive but grow. She smiled at him this time and understood how far his eyes could see.

SPACE AND TIME BOOKS BY MELISSA YUAN-INNES

Space and Time Books awoke at dawn. This August morning had the grey-blue sky of a Turner painting. Though the bookstore had never strayed from Montreal's Sherbrooke Street, it knew about Turner paintings through diffusion. Since books constantly whispered their words aloud, they were soaked up by the store's shelves, windows, and walls, and became a part of it. The books paused only when John Tsui, the owner, came in and began measuring out the coffee. The rich smell of coffee, the store thought, was worth a thousand words.

John pored over the accounts, shaking his head. The bookstore took no notice as John always grunted before his first coffee.

Nathalie came in and shook the rain from her umbrella. "Hello, love. What's the damage?"

"Worse than I thought." He pressed her hand to his cheek. Her burgundy nail polish harmonized with the oak bookshelves.

The bookstore hummed. It liked harmony.

He shook his head. "I can't do this anymore. It's not fair to you."

She laughed. "To me?"

"You can't throw your money away on my store."

She linked her hand with his. "I will throw it where I like, on your store, on supporting you as you write your novel, and on pain au chocolat."

"Nat, this is not a joke."

She stopped smiling. "Neither is this."

He snorted. "Space and Time Books."

The bookstore stopped humming.

"Will we still have our Hallowe'en party?" Nathalie asked. He sighed. "I guess. I have to sell off the stock."

The door's bells rang. It was a girl with black hair and a box-load of books.

"Hi, Maggie. I'm not taking anything right now."

"Aw, c'mon." She dumped the wet box on the counter. "Nathalie?"

"Well, we have Anne Rice...what's this? The Basic Book of Spells?" Nathalie lifted out a book with a black leather cover. It was warm, and she recoiled.

"Cool, eh?"

"Mmm. No thanks." She looked at John. "Sorry, Maggie."

"All right, I'll look around." Maggie came back with a Bruno and Boots book. "How much?"

"Two dollars."

She stuck her tongue out. "Can I trade for the book of spells?"

John nodded his head and showed her a Hallowe'en party notice. "Want to come?"

"Yeah, maybe. See ya!" She dashed into the rain with her box. Nathalie brought out the coffee. They clinked their mugs and kissed, but then the bells rang again.

"Hopeless to get any action here," John said, standing.

Nathalie noticed the spell book on the table and, with a grimace, dropped it in the back room.

The bookstore was perturbed. Finally, a decent owner, books with good vibrations, and now this! Money, the root of all evil...

The store decided to round up some business tomes. They straightened their covers importantly and declared that independent bookstores were closing their doors. Big bookstores were getting bigger discounts, buying up first print runs and returning them, and generally not playing fair.

The Basic Book of Spells lay silent.

"Look at that," a tax book whispered, its spine shuddering. "Someone has to invoke her."

The bookstore called, "With the power invested in me by the books I hold, I invoke you!"

She creaked open. "What do you want, Space and Time Books?" Dust billowed with each word.

The bookstore hesitated. "Money."

"There will be a price. First, you must think of the solution yourself. Second, you may only invoke me three times. And third, you will pay me."

"Done."

The next morning, John drank coffee and fought writer's block on his novel about robots. A nickel rolled inside the door. He handed it back to a little girl. She sniffled in thanks.

A guy bought a postcard and forgot his wallet. John

sighed and left a message on his answering machine.

An elderly woman crept in. "Hi, Mrs. McGarrigle."

She whispered, "I won the lottery, John."

He could smell alcohol. "Congratulations! What will you do with it?"

Her face crinkled. "I'm not sure." He put an arm around her. Her voice was small. "May I use your bathroom?"

"Of course."

John found a crumpled lottery ticket on the toilet tank.

He put it in an envelope for Mrs. McGarrigle.

"It's not working."

"That's not my fault." The Book of Spells ruffled her pages.

"I mean, he's too honest to take other people's money."

"Money has to come from somewhere. It doesn't grow on trees."

"I know." The bookstore couldn't remember which book had said that. "How about...making me attractive to people, so there'll be lots of customers?"

She snorted. "I guess I could try a love spell. I've never done it on a building before."

"Your store is bea-U-tiful!" gushed a woman. "I love the oak shelves!"

Her husband gestured with his cane. "The LED lights are economical yet easy on the eyes."

"Can I help you?" John asked them.

"No, no." She turned to her husband. "Look, sweetheart, stairs! You know what that means."

They chorused, "A second floor."

John interrupted, "It's not open to the public."

A tear rolled down the woman's cheek.

John sighed and took them on a tour. The woman dropped her diamond ring and the man lost his toupee.

Then some kids burst in. "Way cool!"

"No way!"

"Yeah! He's got all the comics in print. How much've you got?"

They dropped all their change on the floor. The dimes rolled everywhere. "Hey! Sorry, man!"

John sighed.

"He's not selling books, he's giving tours."

The Book of Spells' cover curled scornfully. "You got what you wanted."

"I did. I'm sorry. It's just that people are tromping in and losing their wallets—"

"The second spell doesn't negate the first."

"So now I have to make everything right in a third spell, with people dropping money, and drooling all over me?"

The Book of Spells peeled through her pages like a deck of cards. "Got any ideas?"

John awoke and headed to the computer like a man possessed.

Nathalie croaked, "John?"

"Sorry to bother you, hon. Go back to sleep."

She pulled the blanket over her face. "It's okay. I'm glad you're writing your novel again."

"It's not my novel." He wrote until dawn.

A month later, Nathalie was decorating Space and Time Books for the Hallowe'en party with streamers and spiders in the window, and a sign that read

HALLOWE'EN BOOK LAUNCH ME AND SPACE AND TIME
   THE AUTOBIOGRAPHY OF JOHN TSUI

John had blazed through the manuscript and a print-on-demand service bought it. Now people swarmed in to buy, sipping cider as they waited. John signed so many books that his hand cramped.

Later, Nathalie muttered, "It's the Bermuda Triangle of Montreal" as she organized all of the lost jewelry and wallets.

John made a note of that for his book. They grinned and touched hands.

The bookstore was uncomfortable from all the body heat and the spilled cider.

"Oh, quit bellyaching," said The Basic Book of Spells. "I never expected to be this popular."

"Should've thought of better spells then." She blew out a cloud of dust. "You've had your three. Now my turn."

The store's stairs creaked anxiously. "What is it?"

"I thought people were bad enough, but now I've been

used by a building! What's next, bacteria wanting help taking over the world?"

"What do you want me to do?"

"Hide me. Forever." She slammed her cover shut.

"Why don't you cast an invisibility spell on yourself?"

"Are you trying to worm your way out of payment?" She lolled open. "Because I know some good curses."

The store grabbed her and hid her under some cookbooks.

Space and Time Books awoke at dawn. It was December now, with snow and lights on its roof. A street cleaner paused to look in the window longingly. The bookstore touched the book of spells, which pulsed, warm and silent and hidden. The store brushed its uneasiness aside and waited for John to come and brew some coffee.

10

ABOOTASAURUS! BY TIMOTHY CARTER

The Following Are Paid Political Messages

🍁

1. By now, Canadians like yourselves have become aware of an unprecedented situation developing off the coast of British Columbia. An enormous reptilian creature, resembling Godzilla or Kaiju, has been spotted heading North-East toward Vancouver Island. This creature poses a threat to all of Canada, and decisive action must be taken.

Liberal Leader Suzette Charmaine and NDP Leader Elliot Mercer want to observe this creature and wait until more information is available before sending in our armed forces. Perhaps they think it's Dudley the Dragon! What is needed now is strong leadership, for the protection of all Canadians, not hand-wringing and mamby-pamby indecisiveness.

I'm Prime Minister Benson Hedge, and I vow to protect

our country from this monster. Remember that when you go to the polls next Tuesday, and vote Conservative.

2. If you saw a strange animal out in the wild, would your first instinct be to kill it? That's what Prime Minister Benson Hedge wants to do with the newly-discovered marine creature off the British Columbia coast.

Hi, I'm Liberal Leader Suzette Charmaine, and I favour a rational, humanitarian approach. What is this creature? Where did it come from? These are questions that won't be answered by launching a full-scale naval and air force attack!

Send a message to Conservative Leader Benson Hedge. Tell him Canadians want to recall our jets and submarines. And next Tuesday, remember to vote Liberal!

3. The attack on the giant creature, instigated by Prime Minister Benson Hedge, has failed. Now, all of Canada is in danger.

Hi, I'm Elliot Mercer, leader of the NDP. I urged the Prime Minister to let science and reason prevail, and sent a team of marine biologists out to study this creature. Had they arrived before the military, they might have determined that this creature, dubbed Godzill-Eh, can shoot columns of fire from its nose, or that its skin is impervious to torpedo fire. One submarine and both jets were destroyed, halving our Naval fleet and decimating our air force. The remaining sub is returning to port with the creature in pursuit. Benson Hedge failed to protect us from Godzill-Eh, and may have put the entire country in jeopardy.

It's time for change. Real change. Next Tuesday, vote NDP!

4. This is Prime Minister Benson Hedge, and I want to ask all Canadians one question: do you support the men and women who serve in our armed forces?

The Liberals and the NDP do not. They say Godzill-Eh is following the submarine straight back to Victoria, and that our troops, returning to their families after defending our nation from the monster, should attempt to lead the creature further out to sea. Our brave soldiers fight bravely every day, making the kind of sacrifices the Liberals and NDP clearly do not understand. All they want is to return from a job well done and hold their children in their arms. Must they now sacrifice time with their loved ones, on the off-chance they can keep Godzill-Eh from coming inland?

I don't think so. I choose to honour their sacrifice by bringing them home safely.

Next Tuesday, vote for our troops. Vote Conservative.

We'll talk again tomorrow.

5. The attack on Victoria by the marine creature, dubbed Godzill-Eh or Abootasaurus, was both horrific and unprecedented. Countless lives were lost, and the city lies in ruins.

Hi, I'm Liberal Leader Suzette Charmaine, and I want a Canada that is safe from giant monsters. The Prime Minister apparently does not. He ignored warnings and went ahead with an attack on a creature he did not understand, then allowed the navy to lure it right into the heart of a civilian population, where the polls indicated support for the Conservative government is at its weakest!

If elected, I vow to do three things: keep Abootasaurus contained on Vancouver Island; study the large reptilian, that we might know what we are up against; and encourage Abootasaurus to return to the sea.

Prime Minister Hedge failed you. This coming election, vote for success. Vote for change. Vote Liberal.

6. I was really excited about Liberal Leader Suzette Charmaine, but she really let me down when she promised to keep Abootasaurus contained to Vancouver Island. What about all the others on the island? Reports indicate the monster has devastated Nanaimo, and devoured two ferries on its way inland. The entire province of British Columbia is in danger. A fat lot of good Suzette's promises did.

Suzette Charmaine—she just lost my vote. Next Tuesday, I'm voting NDP.

7. There comes a time when you have to examine track records and decide who's looking out for your best interests. I'm Prime Minister Benson Hedge, and I knew Godzill-Eh was a threat to Canada's sovereignty from the start. Suzette Charmaine and Elliot Mercer did not. And the Green Party wanted to protect the creature, claiming it is an endangered species. Now that Godzill-Eh has come inland, it looks like we're the endangered species here. Victoria, Nanaimo, Vancouver, how many more of our cities need to be destroyed before the Liberals, the NDP and the Greens

admit they were wrong about the danger this monster posed?

I have a plan to stop Godzill-Eh, and bring peace back to Canadian families. This *ungodly* abomination will not make it past the Rockies.

If you want a government that will make the right call, vote Conservative.

We'll talk again tomorrow.

8. The environmental impact of Benson Hedge's proposed attack on Godzill-Eh, or Abootasaurus, cannot be overstated. Setting wildfires to lure the creature into a rockfall trap will devastate the wildlife and destroy the delicate ecological balance found only in the Rocky Mountains.

My name is Sonya Fowler, and I'm the leader of the Green Party. Before you vote next Tuesday, I want you to think long and hard about the way the Conservative Government has chosen to deal with this crisis. And while you are thinking, why not enjoy a refreshing glass of Maple Cola? A delicious cola taste flavoured with 10% real maple syrup, it's Canada's cold comfort!

Paid for by your Maple Cola bottler.

9. When I go to get my flu shot, I worry the cure might be worse than the disease. Like Benson Hedge's plan to destroy Abootasaurus. Hi, I'm Liberal Leader Suzette Charmaine.

By now, the failure of the Conservative strategy in dealing with this crisis is evident to all. The wildfires devastated over three thousand acres of forest, and only served to enrage the monster. Instead of being driven into a planned rockfall, Abootasaurus went on a rampage from Whistler to Jasper, leaving thousands dead.

"The creature will not make it past the Rockies."

Wrong! Abootasaurus is stampeding through Calgary as we speak.

"There comes a time when you have to examine track records..."

Exactly! And yours, Mr. Prime Minister, has been a disaster.

I have sent in a team of biologists to examine Abootasaurus. We are analyzing the data. And we will keep this monster from harming our nation further.

Next Tuesday, vote Liberal. Because there will still be a Canada to vote in.

10. If Suzette Charmaine really cared about Canada, she'd make public the data her team of scientists has gathered on Abootasaurus. If she had, we might have known the creature was pregnant, and been prepared when she laid her eggs in the West Edmonton Mall.

Why did Abootasaurus surround the mall with vehicles she'd gathered from around the city? Why does every gas station along the route Abootasaurus took appear to have been torn from the ground? Is there a connection? Is that why Abootasaurus appears to be heading toward Alberta's oil sands?

What isn't Suzette Charmaine telling us? How many more Canadian lives is she willing to sacrifice before she fills the rest of us in?

I'm NDP Leader Elliot Mercer, and I want answers. If you do too, vote NDP next Tuesday.

11. Canada belongs to Canadians. We were born here, we raised our families here. But when others come into our country illegally and take our jobs, our way of life is threatened.

Abootasaurus came into our country and invaded the Oil Sands of Alberta, killing thousands and putting millions out of work. And that's just not right.

As Prime Minister, I vow to remove Abootasaurus from the Oil Sands and give Canadians back their jobs. And I will tighten our immigration policy, so those jobs stay with true-born Canadians.

Liberal Leader Suzette Charmaine says the creature has entered a dormant phase and should be left alone while scientists study it further. Sorry, Suzette, but getting Canadians back to work is not something I think we should wait for.

It's time for you to go, Abootasaurus! And a vote for the Conservative Party will keep him gone.

I'm Prime Minister Benson Hedge. We'll talk again tomorrow.

12. When your doctor tells you to lay off the red meat, you listen. When your mechanic tells you your brakes are shot, you listen. Why? Because they are experts who know what they are talking about.

Like my team of biologists. When they tell me Abootasaurus has entered a dormant phase, I listen. When they tell me a full-scale military attack like Benson Hedge is proposing, will awaken and enrage Abootasaurus, I listen. And he should listen, too.

Further study of this creature is necessary and may provide valuable insight into Abootasaurus's intentions, and more importantly its weaknesses. Study of the monster's young might also provide valuable insight, but Benson Hedge has them quarantined at an undisclosed location. Any data gleaned from them will be kept secret. But in spite of what the NDP have said, I will make all my findings public.

This Tuesday, send the Prime Minister a message; call off the attack on the slumbering giant, and release the information gleaned from Abootasaurus's

babies. Send that message by voting Liberal.

I'm Suzette Charmaine, and I want to save this country.

13. Canadians are tired of being stomped and eaten by a giant reptilian monster. Action needs to be taken to save those of us who remain.

Hello, I am Gilles DeLapin, leader of the Bloc Quebecois. I have a plan to keep all Quebecois safe and create jobs to keep our economy strong. If elected, I will build a solid steel wall all around Quebec, strong enough to withstand Abootasaurus's attack.

The Prime Minister has failed to protect Canada. But we can still save ourselves. Vivre la Quebec libre!

14. Learning from our mistakes is important to strong leadership, but Prime Minister Benson Hedge hasn't learned anything at all. He has attacked Abootasaurus three times, and all he's done is make the problem worse. The assault on the Alberta Oil Sands resulted in a catastrophic loss of life

and caused an environmental disaster that future generations will be tasked with cleaning up.

Survivors of these events are well-advised to kick back and relax with an ice-cold bottle of Moosenberg, the fresh taste of the Canadian wilderness! Please drink responsibly.

And next Tuesday, do the responsible thing and vote Green. I'm Sonya Fowler.

Paid for by the Moosenberg Brewing Company.

15. Suzette Charmaigne doesn't understand families. She doesn't understand the economy. And she doesn't understand how to kill Abootasaurus. She wants to send a small team to inject a synthesized toxin into the creature's bloodstream, and poison him "from the heart out." But research into Abootasaurus's offspring shows no evidence the monster can be defeated by the Care Bear Stare! Our studies indicate that, while its skin is heavily armoured, it is not indestructible. Abootasaurus will be defeated by an air force attack, not a flu shot.

Care-levels are dropping, Suzette! Put your little needle away, and leave protecting Canada to the big boys.

I'm Prime Minister Benson Hedge, leader of the Conservative Party. We'll talk again tomorrow.

16. The tragic loss of life caused by Abootasaurus, and Prime Minister Benson Hedge's ill-advised strategies for dealing with the monster, has been nothing short of horrific. Just as horrific are the injuries suffered by the survivors. These people need medical attention, and with the Conservatives' proposed legislation to privatize healthcare, many Cana-

dians will not be able to afford the treatment they need. The Liberals' health care reform strategy doesn't take Abootasaurus injuries into account. My proposed bill does. I'm NDP Leader Elliot Mercer, and my healthcare reforms will ensure that all Canadians hurt by this disaster will receive treatment.

Don't let the government profit from your injuries. On Tuesday, vote NDP.

17. Abootasaurus is a threat that faces all Canadians, not just the top 1%. Yet in the past week, Prime Minister Benson Hedge has evacuated only the wealthiest people from the monster's path.

Hi, I'm Liberal Leader Suzette Charmaine, and I want to save all of Canada from this threat. My team is working on a toxin, based on blood samples they took from Abootasaurus before the debacle that was the Hedge-ordered military strike on the oil sands. The army and the air force have failed to even slow it down. The military option isn't working, Benson! My team needs access to the monster's offspring, but the Prime Minister has refused. I guess he's been busy sending his millionaire friends to the Abootabunkers.

If elected, I will concentrate on evacuating all Canadians from Abootasaurus's path. She has already levelled Regina, Saskatoon, Winnipeg and Thunder Bay, and was last seen swimming in Lake Superior. Any one of our Great Lakes cities could be the next target!

It's time for a change. Real change. When Tuesday comes, vote Liberal.

18. In these dark, tragic times, it can be easy to lose sight of the issues that matter most. Hi, I'm Prime Minister Benson Hedge, and I want to protect Canada from all threats. Evacuations of the cities in Abootasaurus's path create prime targets for terrorist organizations like Isis. As prime minister, I will see to it that anyone suspected of being a terrorist be barred access to evacuation services. I will also set up a toll-free emergency phone line for concerned citizens to report activities they may associate with terrorism. I urge Canadians to use this line if they feel under threat during any and all stages of the evacuation effort.

Similar policies are being devised for the relief effort.

I want to protect all Canadians. That can only happen if all Canadians do their part. Stay safe. Report suspicious activity. And on Tuesday, vote Conservative.

I'm Prime Minister Benson Hedge. We'll talk again tomorrow.

19. Public transit. Affordable housing. Education reform. These are the issues the Prime Minister has ignored long before Abootasaurus came ashore. And now, while this basic infrastructure is literally being trampled, Benson Hedge continues to turn a blind eye and a deaf ear.

Hi, I'm NDP Leader Elliot Mercer, and I want to fix what was already broken. We didn't need a giant reptilian monster to show us our schools are crumbling, or that the trains are often delayed, or that homelessness has reached epidemic proportions. Now, these issues are as impossible to avoid as Abootasaurus herself.

Tomorrow, vote for infrastructure done right. The Liberals and Conservatives care only about killing

Abootasaurus. I'm looking beyond the monster's rampage, and you should too.

20. Abootasaurus has devastated Hamilton, Oakville, Burlington, Milton and Mississauga. She is rampaging through Etobicoke as we speak. The military and air force continue to fire on the monster but are only causing further damage to the surrounding neighbourhoods.

A change of strategy is sorely needed. And needed now.

Hi, I'm Liberal Leader Suzette Charmaigne, and I am going to save Canada. I have a plan in motion; my team of scientists gained entry to the government research laboratory where Abootasaurus's young are being held and acquired the data they need to kill the creature. There was a reason Abootasaurus surrounded her young with gasoline-filled cars in Edmonton, a reason she took refuge in the Alberta Oil Sands, a reason she continues to devour gas stations and tanker trucks. This link between fossil fuels and Abootasaurus is critical; had this data been made available to my scientists earlier, many more lives might have been spared.

Hedge has failed. My scientists have a real chance at success. Should they win the day, and save us from Abootasaurus, go to the polls tomorrow and save Canada from our incumbent Prime Minister by voting Liberal.

20. Abootasaurus has reached the outskirts of Toronto. The Conservatives' military strategy has failed, and the Liberals' monster poison has yet to become a reality. Prime Minister Benson Hedge promises that a military strike on Toronto

will work. And Liberal Leader Suzette Charmaine claims the toxin her scientists are preparing will kill the creature. But promises and claims won't save Canada.

But the Americans might! The Prime Minister has said in the past that he's an expect at foreign policy, with many friends in the international community, including the United States' president. So why hasn't he asked for help in fighting Abootasaurus?

Is Benson Hedge's pride more important to him than the lives of Canadians? Apparently, it is. But if I were elected Prime Minister, I would seek the aid of anyone who can help us.

Tomorrow, put Canadian lives first. Vote NDP.

21. Hello, this is Prime Minister Benson Hedge, and I have good news for Canada. Abootasaurus, the monster that has terrorized our country for the last week, is dead. I promised Abootasaurus would be stopped, and I delivered.

But while this is a time of celebration for this unprecedented victory, the details of Abootasaurus's defeat cannot be ignored. The data used to devise the toxin that was administered into the creature's bloodstream was obtained using methods indistinguishable from terrorism.

A military institution outside Petawawa, Ontario, was broken into by a group of Liberal Party employees claiming to be biological scientists. Several guards were rendered unconscious, and vital research materials were stolen, including a live specimen of one of Abootasaurus's young. They developed their toxin, no doubt subjecting the infant creature that some have dubbed Little Maple to inhumane research practices.

Then, this group trespassed into a quarantined combat

zone, putting themselves and other Canadians in harm's way, in order to administer their biological weapon. They gained illegal entry to the CN Tower, created a makeshift catapult out of stolen property found on site, and launched their toxin into Abootasaurus's mouth. Their formula allegedly ignited the fossil fuels in the creature's bloodstream, causing an explosion that devastated the downtown core and destroyed a national landmark.

The methods of this team of scientists, while successful, were brazenly illegal, dangerous, and do not represent the identity and values of this country. Their trespass on the military incursion of Toronto jeopardized the mission, and the detonation of Abootasaurus cost the lives of hundreds of Canada's brave soldiers. Had their toxin proved ineffective, many more lives would have been lost. Had they survived, this team of Liberal meddlers would have been punished to the full extent of the law. An investigation into the Liberal Party's involvement is currently underway.

Today, when you go to the remaining polling stations, vote with your conscience. Vote for the government that defeated Abootasaurus. Be a true Canadian hero in this time of crisis, and vote for the Conservative Party of Canada.

11

CANADIAN GODS BY IRA NAYMAN

To be honest, it wasn't much of a mystery, but it did make the endless meetings and paperwork go down a little easier.

My name is Fred. My government designation is MC-5. In theory, *everything* is above my pay grade, in practice... well, things haven't gone as well as we thought they would for the Ministry of Mythological Beasties, not since we hived off from the Ministry of Heritage and Culture four years ago. We thought it was a vote of confidence from the Prime Minister, an indication that Canadian mythological stories and creatures could stand on their own in the world. Given the government's rightward drift–did I say drift? I meant to say sprint, we really should have known better.

As part of Heritage and Culture, the government couldn't do anything to us directly. If they wanted to cut our funding, they had to cut H&C and wink and nod in our direction and hope the boffins there got the point. They never did, as we were such a small part of their overall budget that we were rarely touched, and truth to tell, subtlety was not the government's strong point.

When we got our own Ministry, however, it came with a target on our backs. Every year since the separation, our budget has been pared back. Tough times. Everyone has had to make sacrifices. Taxpayers need to know they're getting value for their tax dollars. Yeah. Yeah. Pull the other one–it roars like a wendigo!

Let's be honest, many Canadian politicians—not all of them right-wing—had been seduced by the myth of Uncle Sam and the Lone Ranger. Well, let me tell you about Uncle Sam, he's an obnoxious prick with a comb-over that only a blind person could believe! *That's* what our mythology is being sold out for?

Um, yeah. Sorry about that. I know civil servants are supposed to be apolitical but it's hard to watch a once-proud organization get eviscerated like we have, especially when Mythological Beasties is so large it's housed in a seven-story office building in Nepean.

The top floor is a specially outfitted aquarium for the country's many mythological sea creatures–oh, and there are plenty. You didn't know? Yeah, yeah, I'm well aware that Ogopogo gets all the attention. Believe me, when Mishipeshu and the Thetis Lake Monster get started on the injustice of it all, you may as well end the staff meeting right there, because it will be hours before you can get any work done!

The sixth floor is our base of the operation, housing native mythological creatures, and the fifth-floor houses foreign mythological creatures who have been brought to Canada by immigrants. There is a complicated formula involving how many immigrants have to believe their mythologies, for how many generations, and how much drift there has to be from the mythology of their native country before they can be represented by MB. To be honest, I get a headache just thinking about it. All I know is, the lady Sif and a nukekubi are forever bickering over who rightfully deserves a desk by the window or the latest computer upgrade.

We used to allow dragons to work on the roof, but the last one was let go six months ago and now nobody has the heart to go up there.

To make ends meet, we've had to rent out the lower floors. The first floor was, inevitably, taken over by Starbucks. The second floor is a health spa and because we don't see many people working out on the equipment, there is much speculation in our office as to what their real source of income is.

The offices of the lobbying firm Huey, Dewey, and Kablouie take up the third floor. This is the most galling, as they represent Longma, Fenghuang, Pixiu and other Chinese mythological creatures. Traitors.

In our office, there is much bitter talk of their presence, but to date, the only thing anybody seems to have done is broken into their office to piss in their potted plants. The only reason I know this is because my boss assumed I had done it and grilled me for three hours about it. The culprits were never caught, but if I had to guess, I would say it was somebody from the health club–they sure love their frat boy hijinks!

We just vacated the fourth floor, so it's currently empty, but nobody expects that to last long as office space is as rare in Ottawa as common sense.

Anyhoo, me. Fred. I'm six foot six and I'm kinda bulky, loose-limbed, and more than a little hairy. My official mythological designation is Sasquatch. A lot of people call me Bigfoot, which kind of rankles because there are creatures with much bigger feet working in this building. Hell, I suspect that there are humans with bigger feet than me working at the gym!

But, uh, yeah, that's the least of our Ministry's public relations problems. As I said, I'm an MC-5, by rights, I should have been laid off in the first round of cuts five years ago but unlike most of the people in this office, I have actual field experience. Sometimes in the bush, sometimes doing door to door research, my experience was multifaceted. That was many years ago though—don't ask why I stopped. I have seen things...done things...smelled things. Don't ask. Still, to his credit, Deputy Minister Jamison, our boss and the only person in the department whose pay grade is MC-1, kept me on because of that experience.

I bring my own lunches to work. On an MC-5's salary, it's either that or sleep in my car but even with the seat reclined all the way, I wouldn't fit. My sandwiches are heavy on the meat, flavoured with the strongest mustard I can find, and light on the bread, to the point where calling them sandwiches might be flattering them, but that's the way I like 'em. I keep them in the fridge in a dark corner of the office, in a bag with my name clearly marked on them. My name, Fred. Nobody else in the office is named Fred because names here tend to contain at least twice as many characters, with many being vowel deficient. I write it F-r-e-d in big red marker on the front so you can't miss it.

Imagine my surprise when, early one afternoon, I went to the fridge and found my lunch gone. "Aww, come on!" I bellowed. I'm a good bellower. Being a sasquatch, I have the lung capacity for it.

"Who took my lunch?"

Nobody owned up. Not surprising, I suppose I wouldn't want to deal with me when I was bellowing either. Still, it hurt. There are many trickster figures in the Ministry of Mythological Beasties, even some characters who would be considered evil but I didn't think any of them would stoop so low as to blatantly disregard office etiquette. Lowering my voice to what I hoped was a non-threatening decibel, I explained this to everyone on the floor. They seemed sympathetic but still, nobody admitted to taking my lunch.

Slamming the fridge door (experience had long required that it be reinforced with steel to be able to withstand just such treatment), I turned to the cubicles in the dark corner where the native mythological creatures worked.

"Nan?" I asked sweetly.

"F-Fred?" Nanabush replied almost inaudibly.

"A word?"

The body Nanabush currently inhabited was slight but looked impressive in a tailor-made suit with a gold watch chain. Nanabush's clothes might make you overlook his tall, floppy ears or the three hairs that projected like wire from either side of his cheeks, just below his nose. His nose twitched so rapidly, it was like watching him flay himself with tiny whips. "I-I'd love to talk big guy but I-I'm working on a-a thing, right now. Major project—could change the way the public views anthropomorphic mythological characters! Right, guys?"

Joe, a memegwesi, Bill, an aniwye, and others working at their computers in that part of the office, mumbled something that could have been misconstrued as support but none of them looked at Nanabush directly. Shoulders slumped, he said funereally, "Sure, Fred. I'm always happy to talk to you."

I led Nanabush into the meagre boardroom with one hand on his shoulder to make sure he didn't turn into a rabbit and try to hop away. Much good that would do him. I closed the door, turned to him and asked, "How are you today?"

"Oh, you know," Nanabush replied. "The bursitis is acting up again. Other than that..."

"Un-hunh. How are the kids?"

"The one I fathered as a man or mothered as a woman? Heh heh. I guess it would be hard to mother children as a man. I mean, where would the milk—"

"Either will do."

"Oh. Okay. "Weeell...I-didn't-take-your-sandwich-out-of-the-fridge, Fred! You-gotta-believe-me! I –"

"Take a breath, Nan. I believe you."

"Wouldn't-do-that-to–wait. You do?"

"Sure."

"Why?"

"You may be driven by your appetites but, at heart, you're not a meat eater."

"Oh. Thanks. But you know, every once in a while..."

"Quit while you're ahead, Nan."

"Oh. Right. Sorry. Uh, Fred?"

"Yes?"

"If you knew I didn't take your sandwich, why did you bring me in here?"

"To show the person who did take the sandwich that I'm serious about finding him."

"Oh. Do you want me to scream?"

"Why would I want you to do that?"

"To show that you're serious about finding the guy who stole your sandwich."

"That won't be necessary."

Nanabush seemed disappointed. "Not even a little one?"

"The longer we're in here, the more time the perpetrator will have to wonder if he'll be next. No screaming required."

"Oh. Okay." Nanabush winked at me.

"What was that for?" I asked.

"Our little secret," he explained and winked again. I could have done without that.

We chatted for a few minutes about Nanabush's sons and daughters and other offspring nobody was sure about.

Eventually, I let him go back to his desk. Of course, I had no idea if he had taken my sandwich or not but I realized that interrogating him wouldn't get me anywhere, so I decided to do what anybody in my position would do, go to a shaman.

The shaman I went to owed me a favour, I'd gotten his son out of a jam with a gorgon once. He gave me a powder that made native tricksters who swallowed it turn red and sneeze uncontrollably. I sprinkled a little on my sandwich the next day.

Three days later, my sandwich had again been stolen from the fridge. Periodically, I would look up from my work, coding oral interview responses for computer input and analysis, and see if anything was happening to Nanabush. Nothing. Except for the occasional wink. I really could have done without that.

That evening, lying on the bed of leaves in my apartment, I considered the possibility that somebody working in the law firm on the third floor could be stealing my sandwiches. Maybe it was revenge for killing their plants, a little late but I knew people who had held grudges longer, decades longer—or maybe it was a way for somebody to break their diet without having to sneak the food into the law offices in their briefcase. Some people think delusions work best when shared with others. Maybe they were frightened by a myth they were told when they were children and this was a way of overcoming their fear–there are some strange characters in this world.

But, no, that couldn't be it. Like most government buildings, there were no surveillance cameras in our office as it was a privacy issue that the civil service union worked out with the government years ago. But I realized there were cameras in the stairwells and in front of the elevator.

A guy in building security owed me a favour because I helped him out of a spot with a dog once, they can be really nasty when they have three heads, but reviewing the surveillance tapes, it was clear that nobody had come up to our floor from the law firm on the days my sandwiches had been taken.

The next day we had a treat, Johnny Chinook was in from the field for a debriefing. He stood tall, his blond hair gleaming like freedom. His debriefings usually took all afternoon because Johnny Chinook had a habit of exaggerating. When you cut through all of Johnny Chinook's BS, a story that had started out being about saving the world might end up actually being about saving a squirrel. He was a great field agent, though people would mostly remember his toothy grin, with more teeth than could possibly fit in the human mouth and a deep voice, and that somehow made any outrageous story he told go down easier.

When he finally left Jamison's office at 4:55 that afternoon, I took him by the shoulder and asked if I could get his help with something. "Sure, pardner," he replied. He must have noticed Nanabush winking at us as I steered him toward the boardroom though, because he asked, "Nan developin' a tic or sumpin'? I always said bein' cooped up in a office all day twern't no good fer a trickster feller."

"Never mind him," I advised as I closed the door behind us. I outlined my sandwich problem. With a grin, Johnny Chinook told me: "Only a low down dirty varmint would steal another man's lunch. Okay, so here's what you do: put laser-guided motion detectors aimed at the fridge into the ceiling. Programme 'em for that there facial and object recognition, and they'll do everythin' but rope and tie tha miscreant for ya!"

"I could never get permission to do anything like that!" I protested.

Johnny Chinook looked at me sadly. "You gotta get back

in the field, Fred. This office is makin' ya soft!" With that, he whooped and left.

All that talk of tech gave me an idea, though. I went down the hall to an office so small you might have mistaken it for a converted janitor's closet. Only, you wouldn't have been mistaken. I knocked on the door, and somebody squeaked, "Come in!"

Inside the room, which was crowded with machines and lit by a single naked lightbulb, sat Kit, a five-foot-tall beaver. He was the last of the Inniscastorium, a breed of mythological beavers that had been popular with the fur traders of the eighteenth and nineteenth centuries, but whose power over the popular imagination waned as the Canadian economy diversified. Kit's specialty was tech support and gnawing wood.

"Oh, hey, Fred," Kit greeted me as he put a half-gnawed stick into an ashtray that was already overflowing with shavings. He didn't even try to hide the fact that he was playing a Japanese computer game involving spaceships and squids on his desktop, something I had always respected. "Computer giving you trouble again?"

"Naah. Somebody's stealing my lunch out of the office fridge."

"You want me to put laser-guided motion detectors aimed at–"

"That's okay, thanks. Just tell me you didn't do it."

Without looking up from his game, Kit said, "Get out of my office."

I was standing in the doorway, unable to squeeze into his office, so technically I couldn't get out of it. Still, I didn't appreciate the hard tone in his voice. "If you're trying to convince me you didn't steal my sandwiches, you're doing a piss poor job of it."

"I don't have to prove anything to–*get out of the way, you idiot!* I don't have nothing to prove to you, Fred."

"Don't take that tone of voice with me!"

Kit paused the game with a sigh and looked at me. "Fred, you know how, when confronted, beavers are supposed to gnaw off their own balls and hand them to the predator that is threatening them?"

"I have heard that, yes." I was a bit mystified.

"That's a lie spread by a member of the Canadian literary establishment I will not deign to name. I don't know why she does that. If there were more Inniscastoriums, we would probably sue her for libel, but there doesn't seem to be much point now. Do you want to know whose balls we *do* gnaw off when confronted?"

I held up a hand. "We really don't need to go there," I assured him."

Kit returned to his game. "I didn't steal your stupid sandwich. Okay?"

"Okay." As I walked away from his office, Kit shouted after me, "Oh, and, next time you have a virus on your computer because you've been using it for something non-work related, don't come to me for help!"

A few days, and three stolen sandwiches later, I was called into Deputy Minister Jamison's office. Jamison was seven feet tall, with eyes too big for his head and an impossibly emaciated body that was not made any easier to look at by a cheap grey suit. He was tucking into a three foot tall and nine-foot long sub, occasionally dipping into a pail full of coleslaw, and sipping from a two-litre bottle of diet soda, while he stared at a computer screen. I've never wanted to know what freakish metabolism forced my boss to eat so much without gaining as much as an ounce, but I thought, and not for the first time, that there must be a way to make a fortune building a weight loss programme around it.

As I made my way to one of the chairs opposite Jamison, I studiously avoided looking at the framed newspaper covers that filled the walls of the office. It wasn't that they identified Jamison as a "windigo" when he had made it clear, repeatedly, and at great length and volume, to everybody in the office that he was a "wendigo." It wasn't that some of the more lurid drawings of my boss depicted the man eating human flesh, when on strict orders from his doctor, Jamison had given up the practice decades ago. No, it was more basic than that, they made me nostalgic for my days as a field sasquatch, something I had sworn I would never go back to after the Derrida Debacle.

"Minister Devereaux..." Munch, munch. "Is very unhappy...mumf, mumf." Smack! "About the fact that she was asked about selkies during..." Sluuurp. "Question period and didn't have a–Mmm..." Munch. "Response!" he told me through mouthfuls of food. When you've worked at the Ministry for as long as I have, you learn to tune the chomping out.

"What does she want?" I asked, the hairs on the back of my neck standing up.

"It's a red ball," Jamison confirmed my worst suspicions. The next thirty seconds involved devouring half a foot of sub, which I'll leave to your imagination. "Everybody is to drop what they're currently working on..." Sluuurp. "And develop a Power Point presentation..." Munch, munch, munch. "Outlining the main characteristics of..."

I could see where this was going. "But there must be thousands of mythological creatures in Canada. Hundreds, if we just limit it to indigenous species, but still..." I paused for a moment, then blurted. "It was you!"

"Hm?"

"You're the one who has been stealing the sandwiches I bring for lunch!"

"Those were...mumf, mumf...yours?"

"I didn't think it could be you because you already eat so much food every day. Why would you need to eat my stupid little sandwiches?"

"They're a great appetizer. I think it's the mustard you use..."

I explained that I couldn't afford to buy my lunches, which is why I had to make them myself. Jamison suggested that I make two, one for him and one for myself. "I could make it worth your while," he said, quoting an outrageous sum of money for my trouble.

Reluctantly, I agreed to make lunch for my boss.

I'd like to quit my job, to say screw this and return to the field on my own and live out whatever time I have left in nature but what can I do? At this point in my life, I'm better at filling out forms than I am at hunting small animals. My instincts for preserving my position in the office hierarchy are now stronger than my instinct for survival in the wild.

Civilization? Pfah! It has killed this country's best mythological creatures!

12

PROTECTING ARTIFACTS IN HEBES CHASMA BY FREDERICK CHARLES MELANCON

The Martians took the three scientists' clothes and threw them in a ventilated tent on the far side of the dig site. The decaying atmosphere of the previously terraformed planet would prevent the Earthlings from escaping. At least, that is what the Martians thought. Marie shouldn't call the inhabitants Martians, after all, they were still human beings. While the term described the descendants of the first Mars colonists, it was derogatory and only used in movies. However, in the last ten minutes, she'd been called Earthling too many times to acknowledge them as Hebers, their chosen name.

While Marie loved movies, she didn't want to be involved in anything that could potentially turn into one. Discovering old science fiction films in the Kroerner Library on the University of British Columbia's campus was what started her interest in archaeology, back when she was a high school student at U-Hill. While sneaking into the university library from her school had taught her how to talk her way out of a lot of situations, those experiences never included placating a bunch of Martians who thought their precious heritage (mostly broken plastic kitchenware and various squishy toy animals) was being high-jacked by outsiders. Just yesterday, her ex-husband, Vick, (now over in the corner entwined with his former-grad-student-turned fiancé) had tapped pictures of the museum in Vancouver where the Martians' treasures would be exhibited. "Even the videos," he'd said.

Her ex didn't care about all the old science fiction flicks. He dismissed her research saying, "Life isn't a movie. No one lives in one." In his opinion, a discarded spoon told him more about a past culture than Marie's films. Anyway, he always thought her videos were too loud. Vick liked to play a game when they lived together in grad school, whenever she replayed her favourite movie, he'd hit her screen's power button before the black-clad villain said that he was the hero's father. On their final night together, Vick deleted every one of her digital films with her attached notes. When she tried to retrieve her movies, the dark screen could only show her tear-streaked face.

Even to Vick, the videos in Hebes Chasma were different. On an encrypted stick of black machinery, personal information, pictures, and even personal footage from the original settlers could be accessed. The home movies were the only reason Marie agreed to go on this expedition. The find would make her a star...at least in her field.

But now, the three of them didn't even have their clothing because Vick accidentally let slip that everything was being transported to a museum in Canada. He didn't bother telling the Martians it was a temporary exhibit or that all would be returned, but this kind of thinking was helping anyone. As she pressed her goose-bumped arms against her bare chest, she kept looking over at her ex and his grad student. Even in the small area of the pressurized tent, she sat so that no part of her could touch the entwined couple. Vick stared right at her. The Martians thought taking their clothes would keep the Earthlings contained while they liberated the artifacts, but they were wrong. She had to escape. The oxygen-deficient atmosphere outside the tent and the gritty dust that covered every inch of her body wasn't as uncomfortable as her ex's gaze and his upturned lips.

The three of them didn't need the oxygen masks if they were quick. While long periods of unassisted breathing were dangerous, there was still enough oxygen in the air to steal a transport. Vick had scattered transports around the site. The vehicles looked like giant popcorn cartons that movie theatres once sold. Marie worried the cartons would destroy unearthed artifacts, but Vick feared damaging one of his precious finds with a long walk. The Martians didn't have the numbers to watch all the vehicles, and they hadn't even left a guard at the tent. To them, the proper Earthlings couldn't handle the oxygen-deficient atmosphere or the embarrassment of being seen out of costume.

"I'm going for the memory files," Vick said.

Leave it to Vick to steal the spotlight. "No, you're not," Marie said.

Still nude, Vick and Marie circled the site to get to the files. She wasn't about to let Vick mess this up for all of them. Meanwhile, the grad student kicked up puffs of sand running to the transports. Her father had been some kind of mechanic.

The locals were at the faded yellow arches the machines

unearthed the other day. If Vick and Marie stayed away from that area, they would go unnoticed. Vick still left a wide depression in the sand as he crawled on his belly to escape detection.

Under a canopy with two overturned tables, a Martian girl stared at a screen playing a movie from the old times. Using a wire from her suit's ventilator, she'd figured out how to access the files. It had taken Marie weeks to learn how to do that. The movie was an old Earth cartoon. In the desert of apocalyptic Earth, there was a girl flying on a walker-like glider while being chased by a massive roly-poly.

Vick threw the girl off the chair and then tried to rip the wire out of the side of her screen. Sand lodged in the corners of the girl's monitor. The Martian kid grabbed Vick's leg. Hopping on one foot, he tried to pry the little girl off and leaning too far forward, he fell on the monitor. The screen cracked, and the memory stick shattered into pieces just as the animated main character from the movie was about to calm the giant insect. The Martian girl scrambled to her device and cradled it in her arms. A tear rolled out from behind her mask and reflected in the broken black screen.

Marie kicked Vick as hard as she could. He fell into her, and they both landed on a table pulling a canvas over them. They struggled to get out, and when they did, the other Martians, alerted by the noise, huffed through their breathing tubes as the two sand-speckled bodies emerged. Clearly, the Earthlings' make out scene had ended.

The grad student wasn't in the tent when the Martians threw the two of them back in.

"Why?" Vick asked.

Marie sat in the corner. In the movie, the girl saved her people and the roly-polies. Back when Marie was a grad student, the first paper she presented at a conference dissected the influence of that film. The paper was one of the files Vick deleted when he left her.. Marie couldn't undelete her work just as the little girl couldn't reconstruct the movie. But this time Vick's actions weren't going unpunished, and in this drama's post-credit scene, Marie promised to send the little Heber the movie.

13

MEDICALLY NECESSARY BY ANDREW JENSEN

Did you know that it used to be a crime to attempt suicide, but not a crime to succeed? Think about it: the legal system had no way to bring a corpse to justice, so why bother writing the law at all?

They've since fixed that little loophole.

It's not my problem. I've never even considered suicide. Well, not seriously. I have a good imagination though and knowing there are all kinds of ways a suicide attempt can go wrong, I'm not tempted.

But, I have to admit, I can work up a fair bit of sympathy for the people charged under the Suicide Prevention Act.

"How are we feeling, Mr. Grundweld?" asked the nurse, in a cheerful voice.

"Let me feel you and I'll let you know." I wasn't being seriously lecherous, but I was bored. I'd been in the hospital for two whole months, and I was getting twitchy. I knew the reason for strict isolation, but I didn't like it. Not that anyone would want to visit me anyway.

"You know we have a zero tolerance policy for that sort of behaviour here," she said, in a mockingly stern voice. She'd been looking after me on and off for weeks and she knew not to take me too seriously.

"Still, increased libido is a good sign. You didn't sneak in any little blue pills, did you?" she asked.

"Of course not!" I answered, "You have a zero tolerance policy, remember?"

"Against self-medication? Absolutely. But you shouldn't need any of those for a long time, once the treatment is complete. If you behave, we might even let you out early and you can go and see how young you feel."

That almost felt flirty! I wonder how I'm looking.

They don't let you see mirrors until the last day.

I've always been glad to live in Canada. The horror stories I've heard about the American medical system have terrified me. Whole families going into debt to pay for someone's urgent surgery? It's always sounded criminal to me. Socialized medicine is a blessing.

Mostly.

Aldina greeted me with a big smile.

"Mr. Grundweld, so good to see you again. You look wonderful! Even better than I expected from the pictures in your file."

"I look younger than my grandchildren," I replied. I

wasn't trying to sound ungrateful, but I had visited them the day before, and it was unsettling. The visit hadn't gone well.

"Aren't you lucky!" she answered. "Not many people qualify for the treatment you got."

That's true. To be rejuvenated you had to have a lot of money for a private clinic or have the procedure deemed "medically necessary." I certainly qualified for that and it looks like I will for a long time to come.

"You really are lucky," she went on. "I have a perfect job lined up for you."

"You actually found something in my field?" I couldn't believe it.

"No, of course not. Your education is decades out of date. I warned you about that the last time we spoke."

"Then what did you find?"

"It's a job at a resort. There's not too much heavy lifting, although you will be running around a lot. You're young again, so that shouldn't be a problem, and quite good looking now, so some of the guests may find you attractive. The job may have some side benefits," she winked as she said this.

"So I'll be a servant. How much does it pay?"

"You'll be *staff*. It pays minimum wage. If you're prepared to live on-site, your accommodation and meals will be included so that's a bonus."

She was right, that was a bonus. Not much of one, but still a bonus.

"Any chance of a higher-paying job?" I asked.

"Not without more education."

"When will I be able to afford *that*?"

She gave me a tight little smile. "Not in this lifetime."

🍁

I was lucky. The resort was on the eastern shore of Lake Huron. It advertised "the second most beautiful sunsets in the world," and I could believe it. The horizon was so vast I felt like I was on the west coast. I quickly grew to enjoy the rolling sand dunes and the swimming. I never got into the fishing and I avoided the water-skiing, but I did learn how to canoe and kayak and eventually, was even leading regattas of guests down to see the ancient pictographs on the wind-sculpted cliffs.

Guests also came in winter for snow sports. Winters were shorter than they used to be, but the resort manufactured enough snow that people could still ski, enjoy the saunas, and a warm beverage by the fireplace.

In the winter I worked indoors, while my tan faded. I remember bringing a tray of martinis to a group of women who looked like they were in their fifties. Martinis seemed to go in and out of fashion over the decades, coming back whenever there was a revival for romanticizing various time periods such as the 1950s and 60s.

These women certainly never saw the 1950s, but they were enjoying playing it. One of them, a "bottle blonde", I think my mother would have called her, made a point of sliding her fingers across my hand as I gave her a drink.

"Your name tag says 'Karl.' That sounds so masculine. Is it really your name?" she asked. She looked like she was trying to be coy. I wondered what shows she'd been viewing.

"Yes, ma'am," I answered. The other women started laughing.

"Don't 'ma'am' me, Karl. Making me feel old is rude, and you mustn't be rude to guests. Call me Cecile."

"Certainly, Cecile. I would never want to offend such a young and beautiful woman." I kissed the back of her hand.

Actually, Cecile looked younger than my late daughter.

My granddaughter would have fit right in at that table, if she could have afforded the clothing.

Over the "oohs" of her companions, Cecile said, "Well, aren't you smooth? I like a man who can lie convincingly. Tell me, Karl, do you know how the sauna here works? I have it booked for a private session later this evening, and I've never used it before."

I blushed. I couldn't help it. It came with the fair skin.

"Oh, I've embarrassed you. I'm so sorry," she said. The rest of her table had gone silent, but I could see their smirks through their stemware.

"Not at all, Cecile," I replied. "I'm finished in the bar at ten, so if your booking is after that, I'd be delighted to turn up the heat for you."

"I look forward to it. My booking is at eleven."

There was a flurry of whispers and laughter as I left the women.

I hated myself.

I was surprised to find I was enjoying myself.

It wasn't a physical issue. Cecile was attractive and she'd kept herself in good shape, but I felt like a prostitute. I'd managed to avoid that, despite the temptation, for years.

"You aren't like the other pool boys I've met," she teased. "You're more grown up."

"You don't know the half of it," I told her.

"Oh, do tell. I love a man with a past."

"I'm not as young as I look," I said.

"Who is? I paid good money for this body. These boobs you were squeezing have been under the knife three times." She smacked my shoulder as I looked at her breasts. "The surgeon is good. You won't see a scar anywhere."

I squeezed again appreciatively. "How does this feel?"

"You tell me."

I blushed. I've never had a poker face. When I'm embarrassed, I can't help lowering my chin, wincing, and tightening my lips. Even my own skin gives it away when I blush.

Cecile laughed.

"I love a blusher! Don't worry, that feels great to me. What we did felt great. And if you'll walk me back to my room, we can do it all over again."

"Really? All of it? But there won't be any steam." I smiled.

"We'll just have to see what we can come up with," she replied.

The nurse was right: no need for little blue pills. It was good to have a young man's body again. It had been a long time. It was wonderful to have no more aches and pains. I did discover one problem though: I was seriously out of practice with pillow-talk.

"So, Karl, why are you so mysterious?" Cecile asked when we were relaxing under the covers.

I shrugged. "I don't talk about myself much."

"That's rare in a man," she teased. "Are you going to say there's nothing to tell?"

"No, there's lots to tell, it's just boring."

"Oh, I don't believe that. You said that you're older than you look. What did you mean by that?"

"I've been rejuvenated. Twice."

Cecile practically crowed with delight. "Really! I wondered what was different. You're a dirty old man in a young man's body."

"You don't mind?" I asked. I hadn't expected her to be pleased.

"Mind? This is wonderful! I can enjoy myself guilt free! I'm not corrupting a younger man at all. In fact, you're practically a child molester, if you've been done twice."

She could obviously read my face. I certainly didn't say anything. I couldn't. I had been trying hard not to think about it.

"Oh, honey, I'm sorry," she said. "I didn't mean to upset you. I was just kidding."

"I have a granddaughter who's fifty-two," I managed to choke out.

"And I'm sixty-eight. If anyone molested anyone, I did. And I had fun." Cecile was smiling. She almost looked tender.

When I didn't say anything, she went on, "If you don't mind my asking, how could you afford two sets of rejuvenation treatments? People with that kind of money don't usually serve tables, even in a nice place like this."

"My treatments are medically necessary."

"That's a good trick! I tried to convince them that my boobs were medically necessary, and they said rejuvenation doesn't work on individual parts. You have to get the whole body done at once. Then they told me that aging is natural: there's no basic human right to a young body. I've never heard anything so ridiculous. So how'd you do it? It'd be so much better than surgery. Are you related to someone?"

"I didn't arrange it. My TiB did."

"Isn't that a bone? In your leg, or arm?"

"No. TiB is short for Trustee in Bankruptcy." I was sure I was blushing this time. My face felt hotter than it had in the sauna.

"Oh. *Ohh!*" Cecile was quiet for a moment. "I'm sorry. I

had no idea. I didn't think there were any bankrupt people left."

"There's more than you think. Back when I was your age a lot of people had huge debts. Some of my friends declared bankruptcy. Then, after seven years of embarrassment, they were free and clear. It didn't make for a good retirement, but at least they weren't being hounded by collection agencies."

"Collection agencies," she whispered. "I've heard of them." She pulled the duvet up to her chin.

"That was around the time the rejuvenation technology was being tested, and it looked really good. I figured that if I could be young again, I would want to start with a clean slate. No debts. Maybe I would even have a chance to build up some savings. A bit of a fortune."

"Something to leave the kids?" she asked, seriously.

"I just didn't want to leave them debt," I replied. "In the end, I didn't leave them anything. They died of old age."

"I'm sorry," she said quietly. "Why did the doctors decide that you could stay alive, but your family couldn't?"

"The debts are in my name. I put off declaring bankruptcy too long. I felt like I'd be cheating people, so I didn't file the papers for ages. Then, when they announced that the rejuvenation treatments worked, I decided to file. I figured I had too much future to spend it in debt."

"What went wrong?"

"They changed the laws. I guess there was too much debt around and it looked like too many people could get off Scot-free, and live forever while the banks collapsed and the economy was ruined."

"That sounds a little dramatic," Cecile said.

I had to grin. "Maybe a little. That's how some news station experts put it at the time. Actually, I was told I had a 'Fiduciary Duty' to my creditors. They changed the laws just days before I filed my papers, and I didn't realize it until it was too late. Ever since then, people who go bankrupt are rejuvenated often enough to pay off every cent of debt. Our finances are put under the control of a Trustee."

"Your 'TiB'?"

I nodded.

"Sounds like a terrible person."

"Actually, she's nice enough. I think they get nice people for that job so none of us kill them."

Cecile arched her eyebrow. "Did you consider that?"

I shook my head. "Not seriously. Besides, my debts would grow while I was in prison. At compound interest."

She shuddered. "You poor, poor man."

I visited Cecile a few more times during her stay at the resort. The pity she expressed wasn't enough to keep her from enjoying what we were doing.

The sex was fun, but she seemed to really enjoy talking afterward. That was when her eyes seemed the most eager and the most hungry.

"You said you have children and grandchildren, but you've never talked about your wife," she said one time.

"What is there to say?" I asked.

"How did she feel when you suddenly became younger? Did she enjoy it? Did she have fun? I bet she was jealous."

I didn't say anything.

"Oh, I'm sorry," Cecile went on. "I never thought. She didn't live to see it, did she?"

"She lived," I answered. This time I was the one pulling the covers up to my neck. "She was younger than me. They like to rejuvenate people around age seventy, so there's less extreme aging to fix."

"Was she my age?" Cecile asked, breathlessly.

"A couple of years younger, but not in the same good shape," I answered. It paid to be gallant.

"Did you stop doing it with her? Did she suddenly seem old and ugly?"

"Of course not. *She* hadn't changed. I had, but it didn't feel like it, except when I looked in a mirror. I was feeling young again, but part of me felt like this was the normal way to feel. She was the same woman I had loved for years."

She smiled at this answer. "I'll bet she did enjoy it. But it would be hard not to be jealous."

"I really don't know how she felt. A few months after I was out of treatment, she started showing signs of dementia. None of us had noticed before. In just a few months, I was forced to put her into a home. First she was just confused and then she became violent. In the end, she was lying in bed, unresponsive. That's what the doctors called it, 'unresponsive.'"

Cecile's eyes were wide. "Did you visit her?"

"Of course" I answered. "The kids did too, but it was hard for them. They had their own children to look after and it's not like she talked anymore. I couldn't pay for a private place, and the public nursing home didn't have enough staff. So I went, every day. She lived that way for almost twenty years."

Cecile was looking the other way. "I couldn't do that," she said.

I tried gallantry again. "Sure you could. You don't know what you can do until you try."

She looked back at me and shook her head. "When my husband had a stroke, I never visited the hospital. He wasn't alone, I hired someone to sit with him. She passed on his messages to me and gave him the gifts I bought. That was the longest month of my life."

She got out of bed and went into the bathroom.

When I heard the shower start running, I got dressed, and left.

To my surprise, Cecile invited me to the sauna again. Clearly, whatever awkwardness I felt wasn't her concern. She was still enjoying herself.

I didn't mind. It was actually fun, once I could ignore the "ick" factors. The "ick" factors being: she was too young and she was too old—but maybe she was "just right." In truth though, part of it never stopped feeling creepy.

When Cecile left, she gave me a big tip. I don't know if it was out of pity or for a job well done.

Maybe it was because I was honest, but the last time we were together, it seemed like Cecile was working up the courage to ask me something. That was strange, since she hadn't had any trouble before.

"What was it like?" she asked finally. "The treatment. What was it like?"

I told her the truth. "It's agony. They do their best to control the pain, but they can't do much or it interferes with the treatment. Your joints are on fire the whole time. Your bones feel like they're being taken apart and re-built, which I guess they are. And what they do to your muscles feels like years of exercise happening all at once. Plus, they make all your teeth grow in again, which means the ones you already have are pulled out first. You can't eat, you can't move, you can't even use the toilet without help...and your eyeballs ache."

I expected her to look shocked or something. Instead, her eyes were narrow, like she was calculating something.

"No pain, no gain," was all she said.

Every penny of Cecile's tip went to paying off debt. Every penny. It was more than that month's interest, so it paid off some of the principal too, which was great, though I still felt like the interest was killing me.

I don't even remember all the things we bought on those old credit cards before all of this happened. They seemed important at the time. I never got them paid down and the companies were so eager to give me more and more credit. I regret, no, I *resent* every penny I spent back then.

Only historians know what a "penny" is these days. I had to explain it to Cecile.

I remember when they eliminated pennies back in the early 2010s. The Americans kept them longer, maybe just so we could still say "every penny" and people would understand, but eventually even the Americans got rid of them. They were too expensive to keep.

If it weren't for public health insurance, *I'd* be too expensive to keep.

That's why I don't try suicide. If I succeeded, they'd just revive me, restore me, and put me in jail. It's amazing what the doctors can do now. My debts would grow for the twenty-five-year mandatory minimum sentence, except for whatever I could earn in the prison factory. That's less than minimum wage, and there are no tips and no bonuses either. I suppose I could find a way to die that would mangle my body enough so they couldn't revive me, but who would want that? I don't like pain, and I don't really want to die. Not exactly. It's just that everyone I grew up with is dead or bankrupt. Who wants to hang out with some bankrupt loser?

I guess you could say I'm tired, except that this young body of mine is full of life and energy. Good thing, too. I have years of work ahead of me. I figure that if I can earn enough tips like the one Cecile gave me, I can be free and clear by the time I have the body of a seventy-year-old again.

That'll be the day when rejuvenation stops being "medically necessary."

That'll be the day.

14

LINGUA FRANCA BY JEN FRANKEL

Conditional release from Defection "Housing," on the condition of this, a live streaming interview with a Francanadian talk show host. Thank God they're letting me do this in American ...

Sorry? Oh, right. The defection itself. Me, I made my move in the middle of "Un Samedi Apres-Midi A La Grand Jatte." I was playing Helena, the feisty and yet vulnerable whore—I'm sorry, prostitute. I forget sometimes where I am. Can you bleep that? ... Great.

Big grin, toothy and genuine, for the camera.

Of course, of course! No more swearing. I'd hate to make your censors stay late because of my American potty mouth. Oh, they're unionized? Lucky them, but even worse for you if I let my P.C. slip and they end up scoring overtime on your dime.

Yes, the middle of "La Grand Jatte," and I was playing the ... "woman of the apres-apres-midi"? Does that work for you? God, I love the euphemisms politeness forces you to! ... Can I say God? ... Okay, I promise the next time it will be in a properly sacred context and not used as a swear!

When did I decide? Well, that's hard to answer, and also somewhat obvious, I guess. Have you seen where I came from? The U.S. of N.A. I know all the funny things Francanadian comedians come up with to recoin the acronym: Unkind Sons of Nasty Aryans, Useless Scoundrels of National Abomination ... Okay, yeah, I just came up with that last one and I know it's not good. But I'm a serious actress, not a stand-up comic. No one goes into stand-up over the border anymore; you know that too, right? Inciting political unrest is a capital offence, and I know comedians here are always joking about dying on stage but ... Yeah, exactly. Dying *off* stage is forever. Pour toujours. Did I get that right?

Smiles again, pretends not to notice the slightly superior downturn of the host's nose. Yeah, buddy, but I'm trying, I really am.

So. Yes. I made a dash into the audience, right in the middle of the second act. Thinking of Baryshnikov, and that he'd have been a hell of a lot more graceful. Made it to the lobby, which counts as "Francanadian soil." As you know. You've all seen it thanks to socialized media ... hahaha, yes, that's probably a joke I should have left back across the border. But it's said in love. It really is. I love everything socialized here. The medicine, the employment benefits, the legal representation if you get into trouble, not to mention the rehabilitation classes. I'm about halfway through the Francanadian history package, in fact, and I can tell you, what North Americans are told is *nothing* like the truth.

Nods seriously, because this shi—this stuff just got real. I'm censoring my own thoughts now! But adoption requires adjustment for both the adoptee and the new parents. And I am not *going back to the States. No way.*

Language too. You know we did "Samedi" in Francanadian, right? I had to learn the whole thing syllable by syllable phonetically, but it was such a great experience. It really taught me to love the amazing synthesis of ... well, you know, of how two disparate cultures can come together and thrive. It's the Francanada way, right?

Pause, because I'm actually getting applause on this turkey of a suck-up line. Big sigh, but keep it inside. I do really love this place. And it's not just because I hate where I came from so much.

... sorry? No, you're not boring me. I guess I'm still somewhat traumatized, although I know I'm one of the lucky ones. I met a young man at the Department of Defection Services when I was doing my intake examination. He'd come up from Mexico State, and he was a mess. He'd walked about four hundred miles on a pair of last century's Air Jordans, and they had him up to his knees in ice. His story? Oh my ... *not God, don't say God* ... oh my word, it was tragic. He'd been sent to the camps after the Hispanic Insurrection, and hadn't seen or talked to his family since. He was only seventeen. How does anyone do that to a kid? And I know, he's hardly the youngest who fled from separation and "cultural reassignment." How do you like that for a euphemism?

Serve? Well, I hope there's some kind of Francanadian version of the USO where I can put my talents to use. I can dance in a chorus line, but don't expect me to shoot straight!

... No, of course, I don't mean that. I know what it means to serve your country or your, you know, adopted country in my case. And of course, I would serve if I was drafted. It frightens me, and I'm not too proud to admit it when I think about the U.S. of N.A. forces marshalling on the Ontario and New Brunswick borders, not to mention across the river in Maine and Vermont. I do pray that your—our—great Eastern border holds firm. Those Newfies are tough!

No, no plans to get back on the stage. Not yet. I mean, doing the last show in Francanadian was pretty demanding, and I feel that as a mono-lingual English speaking actress, it really is my job to get the language down before I take jobs away from native speakers ... Thank you. I'm trying. After all, being polite *is* the Francanadian way.

I hope it doesn't get you all killed.

The End.

15

DESIGNING FATE BY JF GARRARD

Originally Published in *Ricepaper Magazine*,
Issue #19.3, Fall 2014

Date: 05-18-2096 08:00
"Prisoner 8261-GJSD-9578, Ms. Lisa Ling, please step forward!"

The judge's booming male voice echoed through the court. I gulped and took a deep breath. The two guards beside me took off my handcuffs, grabbed my elbows, and guided me towards the prisoner box. Looking up, I noted that they looked like young men except there was no life in their eyes. Their touches were cold as they were androids. For efficiency's sake, robots ran the penitentiaries these days. Humans still ran the court system, though, and my lawyer hoped that the judge would have enough empathy to give me a lighter sentence.

I couldn't bring myself to look up at the crowd of friends, family, and enemies that were probably staring at me. Glancing at the reflection in the glass in front of me, I sadly noted that the orange prisoner uniform hung like a sack on my thin frame and that my luxurious long black hair was all gone. I was a prisoner with the standard buzz cut who had been living in a tiny box for the last two years, waiting for my trial.

"Ms. Ling has been accused of twelve counts of being an accessory to murder in an incident which happened on 06-13-2094. Prisoner 8261-GJSD-9578, how do you plead on this charge?" The judge stared down at me from his podium.

"Guilty," I whispered.

"I'm sorry 8261-GJSD-9578, please repeat, I cannot hear what you said."

Looking up, I took a deep breath and stared into his piercing blue eyes. "Guilty!" I shouted.

Loud chatters started in the courtroom, and the judge banged his gavel before he continued.

"It is noted for the records that Prisoner 8261-GJSD-9578 pleads guilty. We will examine evidence and speak to witnesses before determining the sentence. As she has retina recording capability installed since 2090, we will first be reviewing this set of evidence. Note that at this point in time, retina recordings cannot be modified and the viewpoint will be from her first-person point of view. For the rest of the court, I bring your attention to the digital screens that will be set up in front of you."

As the judge spoke, the guards dragged me onto the open floor and pushed me onto a large metal chair. I bit my lip as I realized my life was going to be an open book with people watching and judging what I had done in the past.

A sobbing sound made me look up. My mother and father were holding tissues to their faces as tears streamed down their cheeks. I closed my eyes and gritted my teeth as I tried not to cry. They were soon hidden as large screens emerged from the floor, covering my view of the crowd. There was a soft click at the back of my neck as wires were plugged into my head. Behind me I heard typing sounds as someone started to access the data in my head. The lights fell dark, and the judge spoke again.

"Let us begin showing evidence from the day of procurement of the 500 Model Series."

Date: 01-13-2093 18:45

"Do you prefer blue eyes or brown eyes?"

The chirpy blonde, blue-eyed sales rep, dressed in a stylish pin-striped suit, pointed to the digital screen on the desk, which was filled with different colour eyeballs.

"Um...blue? Would that look odd on the baby?" I wondered. I turned to Bernice, who was sitting next to me. We looked like Asian twins as we were both dressed in similar executive power suits with our long black hair flowing down our backs and hazel eyes.

"Oh please, blue is so normal. I want purple eyes and purple hair on mine!" Bernice said.

"Of course, Ms. Chan, purple is available for both eyes and hair. What shade would you like?" The sales rep flicked his hands and the screen on the desk changed to a colour spectrum.

As Bernice contemplated the hundreds of shades of purple available, I walked around the store. Designer baby shops such as this one had popped up all over the city for people willing to pay the price to create the child of their dreams. In our case, we were two single executive lawyers who wanted to be mothers. Already in our forties, we had given up hope of finding any prince charming for ourselves.

There were many pictures of babies on the wall, all of them chubby and beautiful. The hair colour ranged from blue to red to black. Eye colours consisted of colours of the rainbow, and one child even had multiple colours in her lenses. Large ads illustrated happy families, radiant mothers, and giggling babies.

"Ms. Ling, have you considered what age you would like your child to be?"

"Age?"

"Yes, there are many busy mothers who prefer to bring home a toddler rather than a baby. In both of your cases, I would suggest a toddler of age five. Our facilities would toilet train the children and teach them multiple language abilities. This way you can save time and avoid unnecessary chores such as diapering or training them to speak."

"Oh!" Bernice sounded shocked. "Wow, no diapers! I was worried about toilet training actually. But if we choose this option, this means we have to wait five years?"

"No, no." The sales rep shook his head. "The children we are creating for you are the 500 Model Series children. These children have DNA sequences that allow for physical performance and growth modifications. The other series allows only for basic modification of eye or hair colour. In regards to timing, we have a patented growth process at our facility that will accelerate the children's growth rates. If you choose to create a five-year-old child, the process will take five months. Their physical and brain development is guaranteed to be better than that of 'normal' children. Also, I was going to ask if you would opt in for extra enhancement options."

"Well, I was reading in the brochure that we can opt in for the healing and strength enhancements. Can we do both?" I asked.

"Of course! Would you like the same, Ms. Chan?"

Bernice nodded.

The sales rep clicked his hands on the desk screen

rapidly. "Can you please have a look to make sure I filled in your child's requirements correctly?"

I looked at the form he had filled in for me. 500 Model Series. Blue eyes. Black hair. Pale skin. Enhanced sun protection skin cells. Strength enhancement. Healing abilities. Extra brain enhancement. Toilet training. Multiple language skills.

Smiling, both Bernice and I leaned in for the computer to scan our eyes for a digital retina signature.

"Ms. Chan and Ms. Ling, a digital copy of our agreement will be sent to your data accounts. As well, please note we will start transferring funds from your financial accounts tomorrow evening. You have twenty-four hours to reconsider your decisions if you want to request any changes. Before you go, I would like to offer you a complementary tool for toddler disciplining the 500 Model Series."

The sales rep placed two plastic white boxes in front of us. Upon opening it, Bernice looked confused as she picked up a small, white rectangular rod-like object. Turning to the side, she pressed a button on it and almost dropped it as a lightning bolt came out of it.

"What is this?" Her eyes flashed with annoyance.

"Ms. Chan, this is what we call a 'Calming Rod.' You see, the 500 Model Series children sometimes don't know their strength and could potentially hurt their normal siblings or strangers. The energy from this rod calms them down and --"

"NO! I will not resort to violence for disciplining children." Bernice crossed her arms and glared at him.

Glancing down in the box, I saw an instruction booklet and a brochure under the white rod. "Look, it's a gift, I'll take it for you in case we need it one day," I whispered.

Bernice glowered at my weakness for free gifts.

"Um, well, if you have any questions, please feel free to

contact us. Let me put these away in the lockers we have set aside for you. Meanwhile, please step inside the chambers to my right for the egg harvesting. We will see you in five months once the toddlers are ready. Have a good day!"

Date: 06-25-2093 09:30

Bernice and I giggled like schoolgirls as we trotted our new strollers filled with toys to the designer baby store. The last few months had been agony. Although we had daily access to video footage of the growing boys, we were dying to grab them into our arms for long hugs and to pinch their cheeks.

The olive-skinned, purple haired, and the purple-eyed child was brought out first in the arms of the sales rep. As promised, our five-month wait resulted in five-year-old children due to the growth hormones option. Bernice squealed with delight as she opened her arms to hug her little toddler. His eyes lit up with recognition and he ran clumsily towards her. From the moment of birth, the children had been exposed to voice recordings and videos of their parents, to create a bond when they finally met.

I gasped when I saw my perfect toddler, with his black hair, blue eyes and chubby cheeks. As he ran towards me, he smiled shyly. "Mommy! Mommy!" he said in a childish voice.

"Mason, meet Juno," Bernice said while attempting to make the children hug. The children grinned at each other and hugged like they were best friends.

Date: 07-23-2093 13:25

It was a beautiful sunny day at the park for a picnic. Mason and Juno were model children as they sat on the picnic mat playing with their block toys.

Bernice and I were busy unpacking the picnic basket when a large growling German Shepard came running into our area. Before we could shoo it away, it had clamped its jaws around Mason's arm and was trying to drag him away. Mason gave a loud cry.

"Argh!" Bernice screamed and beat her fists on the large dog's torso.

I ran over and tried to grab the dog's face in an attempt to pry its jaws open.

Still sobbing, Mason grabbed onto a patch of the dog's fur and pulled a fistful of hair off. The dog let go of his arm as it yelped. Turning his hands into little fists, he punched the dog hard.

The dog flew a meter away and lay twitching on the ground, whimpering.

"What did you do to my dog?" A male voice growled.

"Your dog was trying to eat my baby!" Bernice yelled. "I'm going to call the police and sue you!"

Glancing at the bleeding toddler's arm, the man shook his head. "Your stupid baby was trying to play with my dog! Not my fault he got bitten!"

The argument got louder and louder. Eventually, the man picked up his dog and sauntered off.

"Mommy, is Mason OK?" Juno looked concerned.

"Yes, he will be OK," I replied. During their argument, I had been tending to Mason's arm and noticed that it had already started healing.

Date: 09-08-2093 15:15

"Are you still alive?" my mom's voice blasted from the videophone.

"If I wasn't alive, I wouldn't have picked up!" I retorted.

"Well, you know, there have been all these reports about designer babies being used by the mafia to kill people. Then there are those that kill their parents by accident! It's not the child's fault that the parents asked for super strength and God knows what."

"Mom, Juno is done school in an hour and I have to pick him up. If you must know, the shop gave us a lightning rod tool to protect ourselves and I've never had to use it. Don't worry!"

"OK, just be careful. These kids are not regular people, you know."

"Mom, you are talking about your grandson with your DNA!"

"I guess." She had a guilty look on her face. "Remember, you need to protect him and yourself. If any trouble happens, they usually put the children down."

"Yes, yes, yes, have to go!" I grabbed my keys and headed towards the door. Frowning, I turned back abruptly. "Mom, remember not to go to the casino again! You lost a lot of money last time! And having those loan sharks that show up at my office really embarrassed me!"

She made an ugly face. "It was just bad luck. I'll get lucky on my next trip. Thanks for paying my debt back. 'Bye!"

Date: 06-13-2094 13:00

"I'm ringing the bell!" Mason ran ahead of all of us when we arrived at a house in a suburban neighbourhood. Without waiting for an answer, he reached up and tried to ring the bell. Bernice and I stifled our laughs as it was obvious that his tiny arms couldn't reach the bell.

"OK, airlifting service has arrived!" Bernice handed me her knapsack and she lifted up her son to reach the bell.

The door opened quickly, and a petite blonde woman greeted us. "Hello, Mason and Juno! Hello, Bernice and Lisa! So glad you can make it!"

"Thanks for inviting us, Belinda!" Bernice said as she hugged and exchanged kisses with the host.

The boys ran in excitedly and joined their classmates, who were scattered in the living room. Most of them were boys, and they were playing with blocks or cars.

"We have some presents here for Andrew," I said, presenting my gift bag and carefully taking out Bernice's present from her knapsack.

"Just put it in the pile over there. Can I get some refreshments for you ladies? We have special mommy drinks," Belinda said, giving us a knowing wink.

"Oh --I'm super interested!" Bernice said, laughing.

Our host left us briefly to grab us our drinks, and we walked around the living room, greeting the other parents. We overheard a tall brunette talking to her husband.

"Remember, when those freakish children come, we have to make sure Scott doesn't play with them. They aren't human! They're like animals that --"

Her husband cut her off when he stepped forward to greet us. "Howdy, ladies! Long time no see!"

His wife had a disgusted look on her face. "Yes, you two look lovely in your summer dresses. We're going to get another drink, please excuse us."

We watched in silence as the woman dragged her husband away from us.

"Those racist people! They are just jealous that our sons

are so perfect and theirs looks like a potato!" Bernice stuck out a tongue in their direction.

I sighed. "Well, I think people are just scared of changes. Suddenly there is a set of smarter and stronger people that have appeared on the planet. Anyone that's normal is boring. They're probably just insecure."

"Aha, here you go ladies, two special mommy drinks!" Belinda appeared with a tray of pink cocktail drinks.

Bernice took a sip. "This is so good! Thanks for inviting our boys, we really appreciate this."

The blonde lady flapped her hand. "Please, it's not a problem. I know people get worried about these super kids, but c'mon, they're just kids! Look how sweet they are!"

We all looked in the direction of our children, who were laughing as they roamed around the living room, pretending that they had flying cars.

"That's a cool car! Let me have a look at it!" Scott, a large brunette child appeared in front of Mason with his hands on his hips.

"No, it's my car, you can't have it," Mason replied. He headed the other way towards the other children. Scott grabbed the back of his t-shirt and jerked him back. Making a fist, Scott pounded Mason's head and grabbed the car from the smaller child.

"Hey, give that car back!" Bernice put down her drink and started to walk over to her crying child.

"Don't go near my boy!" The tall brunette lady, thanks to her longer legs, reached the children first. As Mason tried to reach for his toy, she shoved him to the ground. "Stay where you are, freak! You should learn to share!"

"How dare you speak to my baby like that!" Reaching the scene, Bernice stepped in front of the woman and slapped her in the face. The two women started to pull each other's hair and yell curses.

Meanwhile, Juno and Mason ran towards Scott in an attempt to free their toy. The children gridlocked their arms and fell into a heap on the ground. I let out a huge sigh.

"OK, guys, let's break it up," I announced as I walked over to calm the children down.

A loud cracking noise stopped all the fighting. Everyone watched in horror as Scott's nose started to bleed.

"He broke my Scott's nose!" The brunette mother cried out. Grabbing the metal toy car, which had fallen onto the floor, she smashed it down hard on Mason's head. Rivers of blood spurted out from underneath his purple hair. Before she could bring down the car for another hit, I tackled her at the waist. In a flash, the brunette took my small body and smashed me through the glass coffee table before tossing me against a wall. I had stars in my eyes as I saw Bernice smash a cocktail glass and run towards the brunette. I should have had eaten lunch if I had known I was going to get into a fight, I thought as I blacked out.

Date: 06-13-2094 14:45

I woke up to the sounds of children crying. Someone shook me.

"Mommy, Mommy, wake up!" Juno's face was red, and tears streamed down his cheeks.

"Oh…" I blinked and rubbed my eyes. My head was throbbing, and I had to use the wall to help myself up. My son grabbed my knees and I gave him a hug.

"Auntie Lisa, please wake mommy up!" Mason appeared and grabbed one of my hands. I gasped when I realized both of the boys had red stains and holes all over their clothes. Their tiny fists were covered in red blotches as well.

The living room was a mess. The glass coffee table was

in pieces, and there was blood everywhere. I touched the side of my face and winced when I realized there was dried blood encrusted all over my head. A blonde child was crying and squatting over a body of a dark-haired woman. The corpses of parents and children lay scattered around the living room. I heard a crunching noise when I stepped on a few empty bullet cases. I grimaced, wondering who had gone trigger happy.

Walking about the bodies gingerly, I recognized the brunette woman who had knocked me out. A piece of cocktail glass protruded from her neck. Her chest was riddled with holes. Nearby, her husband's body lay with chunks of flesh missing from his leg and holes in his throat.

"That man bad, he hurt Mommy," Mason said, pulling me away from the corpse. "Mommy's over here. Come help her."

Bernice lay still on the floor. A knife was sticking out of her left chest, and the blood flowing from her wound made a river pattern throughout her white summer dress. She held a red toy car.

"Oh, no! What happened?" I moaned.

"Mommy yelled at the brown haired lady. Then the bad man yelled at Mommy. The brown haired lady hit mommy, then another lady came and the brown haired lady hurt her. There was lots of yelling and hitting. People used a bang-bang thing to hurt us, so we hurt them back." Mason had a guilty look on his face. "Auntie Lisa, why won't people get up? They hurt us and we got up."

Looking at the bodies again, I realized that the holes were much bigger than bullet holes. They were the size of Mason's fists. A chill went down my spine. The children must have started tearing chunks of flesh out of legs before poking holes elsewhere.

"Where's Auntie Belinda?"

"She ran out with Andrew, I think. The brown haired lady hurt her too," Juno said quietly.

A sudden pounding on the door startled us. "This is the police, open up!"

"Children get put down..." I muttered to myself. "Mason and Juno, we are going to play a game right now. You are going to find a place to hide, and you can't come out until everyone in the house is gone, do you understand?"

"But the police are good guys! They protect us!" Juno protested.

"Yes, they do, but sometimes they make mistakes too. Did you two hurt some of these people?"

"They deserved it!" Mason sniffled. "They were trying to trap us and used the bang-bang thing on us! It really hurt!"

My son nodded. "They hurt me, Mommy!" he wailed as he wrapped his tiny arms around my legs.

I blinked back tears when I hugged him. My heart was breaking.

"Mommy is afraid of what might happen to you if you get caught. Do you remember where Grandma lives? Hide and then go to her once it's safe."

The knocking on the door got louder. Then there was a loud boom.

I gave both of the boys a big hug and shoved them away from me. Walking over to the crying child, I remember him being another designer child. "Go and hide with my boys, Johnny," I whispered to him. But he would not budge from his mother's body.

"Put your hands up in the air and turn around slowly!" a loud female voice said.

Biting my lip, I turned around to face the police.

Date: 05-18-2096 12:00

The large video screens returned to their resting place in the floor, and I saw many angry people glowering at me. I searched for my parents' tear-stained faces. Mom waved and gave me a wink. I frowned. Mom has never winked at me before in my entire life. A clicking noise snapped me out of my thoughts as I was unattached from the machines. The court's audience cleared quickly as cleaning robots entered the room to do their sweeping.

The guards reappeared to handcuff me and lead me to a small room. I felt exhausted.

During the break, the television blared in the room, and I wearily ate some lunch. An expert on 'Designer Children' was being interviewed, citing that only the 500 Model Series children were defective as an aggression gene had been triggered accidentally while creating the genome sequences. There were blurry videos of children using their teeth to tear out throats of people whom they deemed to be dangerous to their friends and family. I could not help but start crying when I saw children with their hands and feet bounded. All 500 Model Series were being recalled and destroyed by law. Does society realize that it is destroying its own genes in this genocide? My heart stopped when I thought I saw Johnny, the child whom I found crying after the massacre.

Fortunately, the police had not caught Juno and Mason. They hadn't gone to my family and remained missing.

Security entered the room again. It was time for the judge to announce my fate.

Date: 05-18-2096 20:00

I stood up along with everyone else in the room as the judge read the sentence.

"Although you did not participate in the deaths of any of the victims at the murder scene, you deliberately allowed the murderers to go free. As seen in the retina recordings, there were many warning signs of aggression in the children as well as words of caution. You also failed to use the calming rod that the children's designers had given you. If you had been a more diligent parent, this tragedy could have been avoided. Prisoner number 8261-GJSD-9578, although you were not charged with murder, you were charged and have pleaded guilty to twelve counts of being an accessory to murder. It is noted that you have no previous criminal history and have shown much remorse. Therefore, I sentence you to fifteen years in the penitentiary system. "

Murmurs triggered throughout the court as the judge finished speaking. The judge banged his gavel.

"Order in the court! The court is dismissed."

"I'm sorry Lisa, I wish things could have gone better," my lawyer said mournfully as she shook my hand. She winced as security guards put the handcuffs on me again.

The whirling sound of the cleaning robots ushered the remaining audience out. My parents mouthed something to me before they left, but I couldn't decipher their message.

The security guards grabbed me at the elbows to escort me out of court and into the back hallway. This time I felt something odd. Their flesh felt warm and not cold. I looked up at one of them and gasped when I saw purple eyes.

"It's OK, Auntie Lisa, we're going to take you away from this place," the purple haired young man whispered.

"Juno!" I turned to look at the second guard and felt my mouth drop open at my handsome black-haired, blue-eyed son. They both looked like they were in their twenties. Someone must have given them growth hormones while I had been away. It made sense; the police were looking for children, not young men, for these murders.

I stopped walking abruptly. "We can't do this. I've been judged and deserve my fifteen years in jail. We have to respect the law and the court system. You can come for me afterwards."

"Mom, Grandma knew you would say that. She said that you owe her a life debt and you have to fulfill your duties as her daughter. She said that she would be dead by the time you come out and that this situation is not acceptable." Juno spoke in a calm voice.

"If I leave now, what happens? I can't work or --"

"Grandma's figured it out. She controls the Chinatown mafia and the casinos now; she'll find you a job."

"What?"

"We helped Grandma Ling bring down a lot of the kingpins in Chinatown, but that's a story for later," Mason said as he smiled. "Auntie Ling, we promise to make up the two years to you. Really! Now let's go!"

Although some filial guilt started to set in, I refused to move towards the exit door.

"I know what you are thinking, Mom," Juno said softly. "I want you to know that during these two years, Mason and I have been watching the families we had affected. We've been stepping in and helping them when they need it most. We will continue to spend the rest of our lives making it up to them."

Mason nodded. "Auntie Ling, just like how you picked out the abilities and features for Juno, we are asking you to make a decision for yourself. You can either lock yourself in a box for fifteen years or choose freedom and actually make a difference to those who lost their loved ones that day."

The exit door opened, showing my mother standing with her hands on her hips.

At the other end of the hallway, an android started shouting. "Prisoner 8261-GJSD-9578! Stop where you are!"

"Crap, the security robots are coming. Auntie Ling, we really have to go!" Mason's voice wavered.

My mother gestured impatiently with a cranky look on her face. "Lisa, get over here or I'll never forgive you!"

Reluctantly I nodded. "Freedom it is then!"

I yelped when Juno suddenly lifted me over his shoulder and we were suddenly at the exit in a heartbeat.

"When did you gain this ability?" I shrieked.

"Grandma gave us a lot of cool abilities!" Juno replied.

As the three of us ran towards the door with blazing sunlight, I sighed, wondering what kind of fate I had chosen for myself this time.

16

POUTINE, BUGS AND BIG BESSIE BY MELISSA SMALL

P *lanet Axzin*
Toronto Colony
Year 2168

Large stone pillars circled the city spaceport. It was made of red stone structures and situated on the edge of a huge desert planet, out in the far reaches of a galaxy known as Axzin.

Here, on planet Axzin was where humanity met the Drupuzintizti. Also known as Drups, a race of crystal-humanoids. Crystals covered the majority of their body and grew out of their skulls like a great set of crystal antlers. The larger the antlers, the more important the Drup. Similar to humans, Drups also had different skin and crystal tones. The four main colours being brown, grey, blue, and green.

Together the two species, human and Drup, formed the Toronto Colony, a small but important mining settlement. Redtoriam was the colony's main export and a vital component in the manufacturing of spaceship hulls.

One of the biggest troubles the mining operations faced on Axzin were the bugs, which had originally arrived on

Axzin with the human settlers. Back on earth, these insects were harmless, but not on Axzin. No one knew how they grew so fast or why they became so violent but the bugs had somehow exceeded the size of earth insects, reaching lengths of four feet and larger. They burrowed into food stores and some had even taken to eating colonists. A department within the Sanitation Section was formed specifically around hunting bugs and protecting the colony. The jobs of the sanitation workers involved monitoring the tunnels underneath the city and exterminating bugs on sight.

Vanessa and her partner Nerrp were amongst the finest exterminators on Axzin. For years the bugs had been burrowing under the city, their usual exit points typically located by food refineries, recycling plants, and waste reclamations plants, however, sometimes they popped up in unexpected places.

"We found a big one," Nerrp said as he ran up beside his partner Vanessa, holding two small laser guns in his hands. "I should have brought Big Bessie with me. Small bugs the boss said—a handful of small bugs. Does he even know what a small bug is?"

Crouching, Vanessa put her shoulder up against Nerrp's huge blue crystal legs. Nerrp, eight feet tall and with big moose antlers, easily dwarfed the blonde-haired, blue-eyed girl.

"Not his fault. He only has the info from the citizens. And next time we hunt, you get to be the bait." She scowled.

"You know ladybugs don't like Drups," Nerrp replied. "My crystal shell is too tough for their..."

"Watch out!" Vanessa yelled as a beetle sailed over them and into the red tunnel walls. "Pay attention Nerrp, these Japanese lady beetles are either getting faster or we are getting slower."

"Are you calling me old?" Nerrp reached out and smashed his hand down on the three-foot long orange ladybug. He then turned his attention to a bug trying to escape them. "I really want that big one. It would be awesome on my poutine sandwich." Nerrp raised his laser rifle to take another shot at the largest of the bugs, which towered a good foot and a half over the others.

Vanessa glared at Nerp. "Not another Queen. Last time you ate one, it gave you heartburn for a week and I'm not clocking out of more shifts to go and get your meds." She sighed and smiled at Nerrp. "Just promise you won't gut it again in the apartment. I still can't get the smell out of the carpet from the last time."

"I can't promise that, Snow Princess." He gave her a big toothy grin "Let's get this coccinellid bug!" He jumped up and charged down the tunnel towards the Queen bug, ignoring the smaller ones.

"Stop calling me Snow Princess," Vanessa mumbled. Nerrp had many pet names for Vanessa, Snow Princess being the one she hated the most—working underground the last couple of years had made her pale…

She waited a moment, and then charged down the tunnel after her life partner, shooting bugs as she went.

Nineteen huge orange coloured ladybugs now laid dead and two very tired sanitation workers stood over them.

"The Boss will be happy that we cleared another tunnel," Vanessa said as she sat down against the base of the tunnel wall. Red dust puffed up around her as she hit the floor.

"Ah, none of them care. They just don't want another outbreak of bugs like last rotation. If it was up to the Toronto

Sanitation Department they'd close these tunnels up. But someone in their infinite wisdom wants to keep them open."

"I should have been a pilot," Vanessa groaned. "At least I wouldn't be covered in this red dust for cycles on end."

"You failed Cadet school." Nerrp grinned, showing his sharp white teeth.

"Only because of you!" She punched his shoulder. "Ouch!" she yelled after hitting him.

"You'd think you would have learned by now. I mean we've only been together for seven years. Crystal plus flesh equals hurt. Besides it's not my fault that you choose to come and save my butt."

"You can carry your own dinner." Vanessa glared at him as she stood up and dusted off her uniform. She began to make the long trek back to the surface.

"Wait! I can't carry it alone," he called out. Nerrp leapt to his feet and followed Vanessa up the tunnel and left his prize behind him as he tossed the dead bug over his shoulders.

"That's the point," she retorted.

4 hours later

When the alarm clock went off and danced across the table, a huge rock-like hand reached out from under a blanket and with one swift motion picked the clock up and smashed it into the nightstand.

"Not again," Vanessa moaned as she sat up to stare at the remains of the alarm clock.

"Na tif..." said Nerrp.

"You know I don't speak Drup very well," she grumbled.

"Damn alarm! It's probably Toronto Sanitation calling

Poutine, Bugs and Big Bessie by Melissa Small | 147

us back for another shift. It's only been a few hours since we were on shift." Nerrp rolled over on his back groaning all the way.

"Well, that's what we get for being the best at what we do." Vanessa reached for her commlink.

"Says here we are to report to Union Space Port. Better gear up." Vanessa climbed out of bed.

"This better not be another of Boss's test. You humans and your tests. Just let me sleep and then I can deal with the bugs later."

Vanessa looked back down at her commlink. "Not exactly a bug problem this time. Says we had a minor quake and a hole has opened in Union Space Port."

"So, it's a hole; fill it in. Why us?" The big guy stood up and put a new shirt on.

"Says here, that the hole swallowed three personal shuttles and a small inner-city transport. While cleaning up the wreckage they discovered a new network of tunnels. Boss wants to make sure it's not bug related. So, he called his best." Vanessa quickly got dressed in her sanitation suit. She grabbed her knapsack full of bug gear, which included bug detection devices, a set of explosives for blowing up bugs nests, and a first aid kit designed for bug related injuries. She then put on her belt and holstered two small laser pistols.

Vanessa strode towards Nerrp. "Let me check your uniform." Vanessa squared up the shoulders of Nerrp's gray jumpsuit, embossed with the logo of the Sanitation Department. She leaned in and gave Nerrp a kiss. "There. You now look like a perfect Drup."

Nerrp raised his arms and turned down Venessa's collar. "There you look like the princess you are."

Turning around, Nerrp moved towards a large cabinet in the corner of the room. "This doesn't sound like any bug I know. Biggest one I've seen was only eight feet tall. I wouldn't have thought that bugs were capable damage on this scale." Nerrp removed a huge rifle off the wall and slung it over his back. "I'm taking Big Bessie. I'm not running headlong into trouble without some insurance."

"Don't think we will. It doesn't sound bug related. Like you said bugs don't do holes on this scale. Boss just wants us to check out the hole. Well, the tunnels and the tunnels are our turf."

"Lovely," he mumbled, following her out of their complex door.

Both of them boarded the Toronto Centre Commuter Shuttle and were soon flying over the bustling city. Shuttles, personal flyers, and spacecrafts came and went in all directions. People far below were making their way through the streets, lined by the tall buildings built out of the red rock that made up the planet's surface. Vanessa emitted a happy sigh. "This sight never gets old."

Nerrp leaned over and gave Vanessa a gentle kiss. "I know what you mean, my love. It's gorgeous, just like you."

As they reached Union Space Port, Vanessa could see the spaceport landing fields. Starships and personal flyers moved to and fro but covering a large portion of the fields was a huge white tent. "Wow somebody has moved fast. This must be hell on the spaceport coordinators. I suppose it could have been worse though. It could've happened in a residential area."

Nerrp grunted in agreement.

The pilot set the shuttle down on the far end of Union Space Port. As they disembarked they were greeted by a pair of Drup military grunts. Everyone was being questioned.

"State your purpose?" one of the huge Drups asked them. If not for the uniform he looked a lot like Nerrp.

"Sanitation Department, here to map the tunnels." Vanessa showed him her card pass.

The pair of grunts looked at each other. Eventually, the larger one said, "Take the tunnel into Union Port and someone from my unit will meet you there."

Vanessa nodded and they walked towards the tunnel.

Union Space Port resembled every spaceport. It was full of weary travellers, traders, merchants, and pirates. The area around the hole was sealed off, but the station was still running efficiently. Interplanetary shuttles, cargo freighters, and personal spacecrafts were all arriving and departing at the same time.

"Drup military? For a hole in the ground?" Nerrp whispered as he walked up beside her. "I don't like this, we should give this a pass right now!"

"This is our job and besides do you really want Frank and Vat to get it? Remember the last job they took from us? The bonus from that could have paid for real poutine for a week, instead of that freeze-dried crap." Vanessa said as they entered the tunnel towards Union Port.

As they proceeded through the chaos of the landing port towards the tent they came across another checkpoint. Another set of Drup guards examined their passes and directed them towards the huge tent that they had seen from the shuttle trip. They made their way across the field through the crowds of people to a blocked off area.

"Surprised they didn't just shut this place down." Nerrp mused. "It would have been a much nicer visit without the crowds. I hate crowds. You know that's why I chose the Sanitation Department right?"

"And here I thought you followed me. They can't shut it

down completely. It's the only spaceport with interplanetary flights and it's vital for keeping the colony running."

"Still hate crowds," Nerrp grumbled. "So, what's the plan?"

"The plan is the usual plan."

"So no plan."

Vanessa grinned. "Yup, the best plan ever."

There were Drup grunts guarding the tent entrance. "Five guards guarding a hole," Nerrp said. "A bit of an overkill?"

"Who are you?" A muscular Drup guard with red, moderate-sized crystal antlers walked forward to greet them.

"Sanitation Department, sent by Mr. Fox, head of Sanitation Services." Vanessa showed them their card passes.

The muscular Drup pointed at two of his companions. "You two, escort these civilians to the commander."

"Yes, sir! "The guards saluted their supervisor. The one guard accompanying them was a tall Drup with reddish coloured skin and the second had dark brown crystals all over with crystals shaped into a single horn on his head.

Vanessa stopped dead in her tracks after they entered the tent. The hole was about twenty feet wide and sloped down on an angle. It didn't look like any sinkhole she'd ever seen.

"If that was made by a bug. I'm going to need a bigger gun," Nerrp said.

Vanessa looked at him. "If that's a bug hole, I'm leaving this planet and moving to your world."

"My people really don't like hu...." He stopped. "Anyways, what do you think caused this?"

Leaning closer, Venessa replied, "I have no clue and I really don't want to know."

The Drup Guards turned to see why they were not following them.

"Stay close," one of them said.

"Sure," Vanessa replied absently while staring at the hole.

Vanessa and Nerrp followed the guards to a small corner which resembled a command centre. A large table occupied the center. On the table were several maps with notations and pins. To one side of the table was a large gray Drup with a military uniform and a larger than a normal rack of horns. Cowering beside him was a relativity small blue Drup also in uniform.

"I don't care, wake them up! The civilians cannot be allowed to go down there!" The large Drup bellowed at the smaller blue Drup.

"But sir, it's their jurisdiction. The Mayor made that clear. You are…"

"Damn the Mayor. Get me Senator Yali Malvouli and Dumi-talli immediately! I hate politics! Things were so much simpler before the humans."

"Brigadier General, these are the…" Their escort was cut off before he could finish.

"I'm not allowing you in," The Brigadier said as he turned around to face them. He was a huge Drup with glowing gold eyes and a chest full of awards and decorations from the Drup military. "This is a Drup military matter."

"Under this city is our jurisdiction and if you don't like it, you can take it up with the mayor's office, but it sounds like you already have. So, we'll be on our way." Vanessa turned, grabbing Nerrp's arm.

Vanessa stormed out of the tent pulling Nerrp behind her. "Oooo, those kinds of guys really get me upset. You see his face when I told him we were in control. It was priceless!" She smirked.

Brushing past the guards Nerrp told them, "Everything is good, guys! We're going down."

A moment later they found themselves underground, but it didn't feel like the regular red tunnels they were used to. The tunnels were darker red in colour, with less sand and more gravel. Vanessa pulled out her commlink which had a map app. "I'm going to start mapping the area to see what is ahead of us, so we don't get lost in this labyrinth,"

"Weird! Why is there a Brigadier General assigned to a hole in the ground?" Nerrp pondered. "You know it won't be long before he follows us down here. So, we better make this quick."

"I'm surprised my little speech worked."

"I think you caught him by surprise. You are good at that."

"Thanks." Vanessa studied the map app. "HUH?"

"Huh good or huh bad?"

"I'm not sure. There is an anomaly in the readings. It's ahead about five hundred meters, it says it's at a slight turn at the junction and then left. There is something there but I can't get an exact reading."

"Well let's go see what lurks in the shadows?" He drew Bessie off his back and brought it around to hold it at the ready.

"You had to say that," Vanessa said as she followed him.

The tunnels twisted and turned as they walked. If not for her commlink they would have been lost. The tunnels all had the same dark red gravel spread along the floor and the dark red stone walls were carved out of the rock by something both of them had never seen before. The passageways were smooth and round. Vanessa kept her eyes on the device while Nerrp kept an eye out for trouble.

As he turned the last corner, Nerrp saw something shiny. "What is that?"

Drups had fantastic eyesight in low light but he was having trouble seeing whatever it was in front of them. "There is something wrong with that wall. See how it curves towards the ceiling." Pointing at the wall, he continued, "It's not natural." As they drew closer they suddenly realized the shiny object was a starship door.

"A starship underground?" Vanessa was surprised. "It must have been here for centuries?"

Nerrp shook his head. "Nope that's impossible. This outpost hasn't been around that long. It was only built one hundred and fifty years ago."

"Maybe the earthquake made it sink?"

"Don't know but let's go inside and see what the flight recorder says." Nerrp walked up to the door and hit it with his fist. Nothing happened except his mouth went off, spewing foul words, as the bones in his hands cracked.

"Oh, for crying out loud Nerrp." Vanessa rolled her eyes. She walked over and began moving her hands around the door frame, probing the soft sand that made up the wall.

After a few minutes of moving small amounts of red powdery dust and small rocks out of the way, she found an access panel. She removed her multi-tool from her belt and dug around the panel to open the latch. She almost had it all the way out when she heard a rumble from the inside of the ship and the door slid open.

Standing in the middle of the doorway was an old droid. It was tall with a tiny headset on a square body with two very skinny legs. Its body was covered in mismatched metal plates. It looked like it had been using parts of other droids to keep itself working. The droid just stood in the ship's doorway, looking at them. Its tiny head could hardly move back and forth without its parts squealing loudly.

Nerrp glanced over at her and then at the droid. "Well, looks like we found the way in."

"Vriki Liku Jijij P," the droid looked at Nerrp for instructions.

"Was that Drup? Nerrp, do you understand it?" Vanessa asked.

"It's speaking in the old tongue. Man, what I would give to ask my Grum Stone right now." He replied back to the droid in his best Old Drup. "Gyivionuiop!" The droid looked at Vanessa, paused for a second, and then it raised its arms up and pointed them at her. Two weak laser beams emitted from its hands.

Vanessa dove to the floor. There wasn't very much space in the tunnel to be dodging firing weapons.

Nerrp lunged for the droid, wrapped his hands around its head, and pulled it clean off. In a frenzy, he started pulling parts off the droid through the hole in its neck and continued to tear it to pieces until the body fell over. Nerrp placed his foot on what was left of it and yelled back. "All clear Princess!"

"Next time Nerrp," Vanessa said as she stood back up, brushing the dirt off her jumpsuit, "I do the talking. You suck!"

"Hey, it's not my fault!"

"Forget it. Let's go see what this ship is doing here but you owe me dinner at Hortons!"

The two peeked inside the ship's doorway to make sure there were no more deadly robots. Seeing the coast was clear, they made their way down the dimly lit corridor towards what they hoped would be the bridge. A few wrong turns later, they found a mess hall, a rec room of sorts and a few storage areas, as well as a make-shift mechanics bay where they believed the droid had been doing the repairs to himself. Although it had been underground so long, the droid had kept the ship rather clean. After touring the ship, they finally found the bridge a few doors down from the mechanic's room.

Vanessa began to examine all the controls. "Good thing I'm a pilot,"

"You're not a pilot, you didn't make the grade, Princess."

"Ah, they just didn't like my landings," she said as she pushed a button. The lights brightened to full power. "I knew it was on reserve power! All the controls look like they are written in Drup. That confirms it, this is one of your people's ships."

"It's old!" Nerrp exclaimed. "I've only seen this type of ship once in a gorvtion,"

"A what?" Vanessa questioned.

"Sorry, a museum. But these ships were abandoned over one hundred and fifty years ago or more. Back when the Mark IV Faster than Light Engines came into production. These ships couldn't handle the strain the Mark IV's put on their frame."

"We got here about that time, from Earth," Vanessa replied. "At least that's what we were told in history class as children. They said the Drups rescued us. Our ship was lost in space and they helped us find this planet safely. Then the Drups helped our ancestors found the colony here."

"Can you get the systems up and running so we can look at the logs?"

"I'm not sure. It's in your language and my Drup is not that good," she said as she looked around the system to see what she could find. "Wait, there is a file here that's not in Drup, let me pull it up."

"Is that in old English?" Nerrp asked. "What is a human file doing on a Drup ship?"

"It reads…" Before she could answer him, the screen turned off and the lights dimmed to their previous intensity.

Vanessa tried to call up the screen again but she was locked out.

Standing in the doorway of the bridge was the Brigadier General and two of the heavy armoured guards. The General spoke directly to Nerrp. "Lieutenant Nerrp, this ship is off limits to humans, remove her from my sight."

"I don't serve the Corp anymore and this human is my mate," Nerrp replied angrily. "What are you up to?"

"Kidnapping, planetary attacks, and raids on lesser-known worlds," Vanessa responded, looking up from the glowing screen she managed to reactivate. "You took my people from Earth. There was no rescue. The Drups kidnapped my ancestors and they were going to use humans as slaves but we rebelled. During the revolt, this navigation unit was damaged and the ship crashed here. You have hidden this well in the history books. I wonder why my people never talk about this?" Vanessa paused thoughtfully and then added, "If word of this gets out that your people were attacking younger worlds. Man, this could cause disgrace for your kind in the Galactic Senate. Your people would lose trade and maybe even be arrested for treason."

Rage crossed the Brigadier Generals face. "My people settled these stars before your people climbed out of the ooze of your planet's depths. We elevated other species and brought them to the stars. We showed them the universe."

"Yeah, as slaves. You have built your empire on the backs of the lesser races. I wouldn't be surprised if you are still doing it now out on the fringes!" Vanessa roared.

"We needed many hands to build our glorious empire and now it's all crumbling apart. The politicians and diplomats give the orders now. We are ordered to work with the inferior races! And to take a lesser race to be one's mate…" The Captain spat the last words at Nerrp and then brought his attention back to Vanessa. "It all started going wrong when your people crashed this ship."

"Well," Nerrp said. "Guess we'll be leaving now, Mr. Crazy Drup." He turned and grabbed Vanessa's hand, all the while keeping Bessie aimed at the General.

"We shall make sure you both never see the top-side again. I cannot allow you to tell the tale we have so carefully guarded through the years. I have my orders, the secret will remain buried."

The Brigadier commanded. "Kill them both!"

Nerrp and Vanessa raised their guns and began shooting.

ABOUT THE EDITORS & AUTHORS

About The Editors

JF Garrard – Editor, *Designing Fate*

JF is the founder of Dark Helix Press, Co-President of the Toronto Branch of the Canadian Authors Association – Toronto, Deputy Editor for *Ricepaper* Magazine and Assistant Editor for *Amazing Stories* Magazine. She is an editor and writer of speculative fiction (*Trump: Utopia or Dystopia, The Undead Sorceress*, non-fiction (*The Literary Elephant*). Her short stories The Metamorphosis of Nova is included in the *Blood Is Thicker* anthology by Iguana Books; The Perfect Husband is in the *We Shall Be Monsters* Frankenstein anthology by Renaissance Press and upcoming The Curse will be published in an upcoming Brave New Girls Anthology. jfgarrard.com

Sarah WaterRaven – Editor

Author of the *Detective Docherty* series and publisher of the fantastic and miscellaneous, Sarah WaterRaven loves to write books. Ruled by an overpowering imagination, when she is not writing she is often drawing, painting or pretending to play the violin—she wishes she could fiddle. Forever fueled by copious amounts of espresso and tea, she practices yoga and cycles whenever she can. sarahwaterraven.com

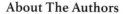

About The Authors
Timothy Carter – *Abootasaurus*

Timothy Carter is a writer of far-fetched fiction for young adults and the young at heart (and mind). Born in England during the week of the final lunar mission, he has a great love of outer space and tea. Timothy is the author of *The Five Demons You Meet in Hell, Epoch, Evil?, Apoca-Lynn* and *Section K*. He lives and writes in Toronto with his cat. Feel free to visit his Facebook Page & Author Site timothycarterauthor.wordpress.com.

Jen Frankel – *Lingua Franca*

Jen is the author of the *Blood and Magic* series about young heroine Maggie Stuart. The first two books in the series, *The Last Rite* and *The Red Ring*, deal with Maggie at ages 13 and 16 respectively. The third (and penultimate), *Heaven and Hell*, will feature Maggie at age 23, living in Montreal and still struggling with her powers. Her podcast, *Jen Frankel Reads Random S#it!* is a great resource for all writers. Jen is also an avid screenwriter and an award-winning poet, as well as a great lover of fish, birds, cats, and all other living creatures. She even has a soft spot for human beings, provided they behave at least as well as their pets. jenfrankel.com

Mathias Jansson – *Sell Off*

Mathias Jansson is a Swedish art critic (AICA-member) and poet. As an art critic he is mainly focused on new media art and specially Game Art, i.e contemporary art inspired by video games. He is a writer for Swedish and international magazines and blogs as *DigiMag, Gamescenes, Konsten.net* and *Konstperspektiv*. mathiasjansson72.blogspot.se

Andrew Jensen – *Here Comes Santa Claus & Medically Necessary*

Andrew Jensen lives in Braeside, Ontario. He is a United Church minister and Kermit the Frog impersonator, who has played trumpet with a semi-pro jazz band. He's a regular in local musical theatre productions. Andrew's most recent stories are published in *Abyss & Apex* magazine, and the anthology *Tales from the Fluffy Bunny*. You can find him at Linked-In.

Ira Nayman – *Canadian Gods*

IraNaymanisaTorontohumouristwho...forgets to use spaces when he gets excited about a project. He has had six humorous SF novels published by Elsewhen Press, the most recent of which is *Good Intentions: The Alien Refugees Trilogy: First Pie in the Face*. His tenth collection of satirical news from alternate realities, *Angels of Our Bitter Nature,* has appeared on Amazon; by the time you read this, book10.5 of the Alternate Reality News Service Series, *Idiotocracy for Dummies*, may also be available. He is the Editor of Amazing Stories Magazine. New humour is published weekly on Ira's Web site, *Les Pages aux Folles* (http://www.lespagesauxfolles.ca).

Helen Power – *The Night Librarian*

Helen is a librarian, writer, and fridge magnet connoisseur living in Windsor, Ontario. In her spare time, she haunts deserted cemeteries, loses her heart to dashing thieves, and cracks tough cases, all from the comfort of her writing nook. Her website is helenpower.ca. Follow her on Instagram @powerlibrarian, on Twitter @thesula, or check out her bookish blog about the strange and unexplained at biblioccult.wordpress.com

Frederick Charles Melancon – *Protecting Artifacts in Hebes Chasma & Making Waves*

Frederick Charles Melancon is a native of New Orleans, but he currently lives in Mississippi with his wife and daughter. He is often surprised how every river reminds him of the Mississippi River, and it doesn't matter how far he is from home.

Christine Rains – *Mother of Caribou & Carnaval Stream*

Christine Rains is a writer, blogger, and geek mom. She was born and raised in Canada, but married an American and moved to southern Indiana. She misses the snow and the donuts. She's a proud member of Untethered Realms and S.C.I.F.I. She has one novel and several novellas and short stories published.

Website: christinerains.net, Blog: christinerainswriter.blogspot.com

Melissa Small – *Poutine, Bugs and Big Bessie*

She's a mother first of two boys and has a husband that shares all her nerdy hobbies. A member of the Star Wars 501st Canadian Garrison, she would love to write a Star Wars book someday. She also loves and trains Appaloosa horses.

Ryan Toxopeus – *Carbon Concerns*

Ryan Toxopeus, award winning writer of the Empire's Foundation fantasy trilogy, has been writing fantastic tales for two decades. He has published two novels (*A Noble's Quest*, *A Wizard's Gambit*), two novellas (*Demon Invasion*, *Dangers of Tensire*), several short stories related to his larger fantasy world, and other stand-alone stories including *Macimanito Môswa* which won Honourable Mention in the L. Ron Hubbard Writers of the Future contest.

Website/Blog: prcreative.ca/ryan

Amazon: amazon.com/Ryan-Toxopeus/e/B0095WNDXK

Paul Williams – *Her Last Walk*

Paul Williams is a British author living in Australia. He is best known for his third non-fiction book, a study of 333 Jack the Ripper suspects. This is his 58th short story. You can find out more at https://paulecwilliams.org

Melissa Yuan-Innes – *Space and Time Books*

Melissa Yuan-Innes is a Writers of the Future Award-winning writer of fantasy and science fiction and, under the name Melissa Yi, a Derringer and Arthur Ellis Award finalist author of medical mysteries. She is also an emergency physician with one husband, two small children, and one rescue Rottweiler. Say hi to Melissa Yi Yuan-Innes on Facebook and @dr_sassy on Twitter, or sign up for a free book at www.melissayuaninnes.com

Made in the USA
Middletown, DE
09 April 2023